CW00548324

Storm

Daughters of Doom, Volume 1

Jamie Spicer

Published by Jamie Spicer, 2023.

Acknowledgements:

MOM: Storm is about strong women. Thanks for showing me how to be strong. I love you.

Samantha: You are always there to keep me motivated, always there to be a cheerleader. You are one of a kind my girl, never change. Thank you.

Cassandra: I don't know what I would do without your smart mouth and your cuntiness. Thanks for being such a good friend.

Ayden: You are so amazing!! Without you Storm wouldn't be as awesome as it is. Thank you for everything you do for me. You have no idea how much it means to me.

Brookie: Thank you for bringing your keen eye, and laughter into my life. Also, thank you for beta reading my books for me. I appreciate it mucho grande.

Courtney: Thank you for always being in my corner. Thanks for always supporting in everything I do. I love you.

Tails the Fox: Thanks for being my bestest friend.

Dear Reader,

THANK YOU FOR TAKING a chance on me. I truly appreciate every read, every review and every page turned on KU. Without you readers, us author's wouldn't matter.

THIS BOOK HAS SOME dark situations that may not be suitable for everyone. If you want a list of trigger warnings you can find them on my website http://jamiespiceauthor.com[1]

If you spot any problems with the book such as grammatical errors or a plot hole or you have questions email me at jamiespiceauthor@gmail.com.

---

1. https://jamiespiceauthor.godaddysites.com/

Thank you for reading,
Jamie XOXO

Dedication:

THIS BOOK IS DEDICATED to the survivors. To the ones that only dream of being able to take matters into their own hands. To the women who had been dealt a sucky hand at life, but who are stronger for it. To those who have been down and out, but dug themselves out. I see you, you strong bitch, I see you!

Glossary:

CRONE- The ol' lady (girlfriend or wife) of a member of the Murder of Crows Motorcycle Club.

Crowettes- the club women. Women who frequent or live at the clubhouse who do sexual favors for the members.

Church- Meetings for the club members

Cage-A truck, car, van. Something other than a motorcycle

Cut (kutte)- a leather vest with the club's logo and patches of rank.

Music Playlist ◈

1) ADDICTED- SAVING Abel
    2) Blank Space- I Prevail
    3) Whore- In this Moment
    4) Bad out of Hell- Meatloaf
    5) I Get Off- Halestorm
    6) Jealous- Nick Jonas
    7) Crazy Bitch- Buckcherry
    8) I'll Follow You- Shine down
    9) Son of a Sinner- JellyRoll
    10) Fuck Away the Pain- Divide the Day

Chapter 1: Kelsey

Then Ten years old

This whole summer Talon has snuck me away to teach me about bikes. He's let me drive and has even shown me how to take care of it. Those days are my favorite. I love learning all I can and that feeling of power between my legs as the wind whips my hair back. At ten years old, I know who I want to be and what I want in my life and I'm going to do it, no matter what.

What I'm *not* going to be is anything like my momma. I ain't going to be passed from man to man and used for sex like the club whore she is. My dad was a club member, who got sent to prison for murder and my mother and I were left to the so-called protection of the Crows. We aren't though unless you call my mom being used as a fuck toy and me being used as a maid, protection. The day my dad got a life sentence was the day my life turned to complete hell and just kept getting worse the older I got.

One night after a party at the club, I walked in on my mother and four guys fucking. From that moment on, I knew I was going to get away from the Crows and I would not follow in my mother's footsteps. The worst thing about my mother, she enjoyed being club pussy. She loved what the nasty men did to her, the grease-stained, calloused hands all over her, their body funk polluting the air. I guess it helps her forget that she is worthless and maybe even forget she's a mother. It made my stomach churn just thinking about it, about the slimy men, about my whore of a mother.

Talon, the son of the president of the Murder of Crows Motorcycle Club, is my only friend. After school, we go far away from the clubhouse into a clearing in the woods where he teaches me how to ride his motorcycle. It's not a full-size bike, it is a beginner one. A dirt bike since he's only ten but had started learning to ride, before he could walk. We have to hide out because his dad will beat him if he finds out that Talon is letting a bitch drive his motorcycle instead of riding. "Bitches don't drive, they ride. That is why the bitch seat was invented," is what Talon's dad says, all the time.

"I'm only teaching you how to drive it because when you're eighteen, you're going to be my Crone," Talon says, as he gives me a smirk. "You don't have to be good at it since you're just going to ride behind me in the bitch seat anyway, but I may need you to grab it for me or work on it when I ask you to. My mom doesn't know shit about bikes and my dad is always complaining about it, but you will be different." A Crone is the motorcycle club's wives or girlfriend, their ol' lady. Why don't they just call them their wife or girlfriend? Heck, if I know.

"Talon. Keep dreaming! I'm never going to be your ol' lady. I'm not going to ride bitch either, but hop on and you can ride with me," I say, as I slam, the kickstart causing the bike to roar loudly. "I won't tell anyone you rode bitch seat."

I know it would make the other kids bully him if they were to ever find out. Murphy and the twins Cash and Price, always pick on him for hanging out with me. Their dads are members of the club, too, so they think they are so cool. He knows I'll keep it just between me and him which is why he trusts me so much. He just smiles, climbs on the bike, and kisses my cheek.

I have no interest in being an ol' lady or a bikers' bitch. What I really want is to ride my own motorcycle and I refuse to be a club girl. Talon is my best friend, but he doesn't know I want to move away and leave as soon as I can. That's something I keep locked up tight within my heart.

Chapter 2: Talon

Then Twelve years old

I love sneaking away with Kelsey. Her long brown hair is always in a ponytail and when we ride it hits me in the face smelling of oranges or when I tell her she is going to be my ol' lady one day, she gets a big smart mouth. She's the only girl I can stand to be around. What I love most is that she isn't into Barbie dolls and make-up like most girls. No. Kelsey likes the same things as me. Motorcycles, horror movies, superhero comics especially, the Batman ones. And when she gets hurt, Kelsey never cries and she'll also pay close attention when I'm teaching her about riding. There's nothing I don't love about being around her.

My dad wants me close to the clubhouse or working in the garage with Uncle Miller. He isn't my real uncle, but he is my dads brother by choice. I have a lot of uncles. On days when my dad is busy with *"club business"* I sneak away to be with Kelsey. She's my best friend, well my only *one* really. No one at school likes bikers. Everyone considers us trash or dirty, which suits me just fine. I don't want to be friends with a bunch of stuck up cunts anyways. Besides, hanging out with Kelsey is way better than hanging out with anyone else.

"KELS, HOP ON," I HOLLER, one Sunday afternoon while my dad is in church.

It's the club's church. Not like going to a religious church, it's more of a meeting the club has every Sunday that's for private members only. Every time I ask what they talk about in church my dad will only say, *"club business son, you will find out when you're older."*

"OKAY." SHE GRABS ONTO my shoulders, swinging her leg over and crawls behind me, wrapping her tiny arms around me.

I take off my helmet, handing it to her. I'm thankful she doesn't give me any fuss because I can't have her getting hurt. If anything were to happen, it would not only make me sad, but dad would kill me for letting her on my bike. She grabs the helmet from my grasp and tightens the straps like she has done many times before. I don't understand why I like Kelsey on my bike or why we just click, but we do. I just know I can enjoy this with her forever and at twelve years old that is pretty special.

We spent the whole summer together. Every single free minute, we try to sneak away and spend time together, both of us riding our bikes, talking, and swimming in the lake. Kelsey is my best friend and this is one of the best summers of my life.

Chapter 3: Storm

Now Twenty-seven years old

"Mr. Davenport open your fucking eyes!" I snarl, punching the fat bastard in the mouth, causing blood to gush from it and spray on my t-shirt and leather cut.

"Bear, pour water on his face. Let's wake this fucker up." I take my eight inch blade and slice his arm causing more blood to run and trickle onto the floor. Bear, the Daughters of Doom treasurer, splashes cold water from a bottle in his face.

Of all my council members, Bear is the brightest when it comes to numbers, most of us never finished high school let alone graduated college. Bear is a bad ass too, don't get me wrong. She's an excellent marksman and there isn't a target that the bitch can't hit. But, her specialty is in numbers and keeping the books for all the club's businesses.

"Wakey-wakey, you fat pervert," she coos, with a grin on her sweaty face, the back of her hand brushing her black hair out of her eyes. "The weather is fucking hot today. This killing room is a million damn degrees," she complains.

The killing room *is* hot. It's located in the deepest part of the woods in a cabin, close to our clubhouse.

Siren, the Daughters of Doom enforcer, standing six feet and two inches tall and weighing about one hundred eighty pounds, treads over to the man we have tied up.

Siren's built like the proverbial brick shithouse and has nothing but curves and sex appeal. Not only is she one of the baddest bitches I've ever known, but she is crazy as fuck, which helps in the business we do. She's a minx, a vixen, that lures in our targets with a hair flip and a smile. That's how she got her roadname. She coaxes men to their deaths just like the ethereal sea creatures do to seamen. Siren will never take anyone's shit and will never be a doormat. Well, never again, that is.

Siren carries a beige folder with his name scrawled on the front and begins pulling out seventeen pictures of children from the ages of two to twelve that this child rapist and killer is known for molesting. The fact that he's still allowed to walk around, still granted his *fucking* freedom is beyond me.

Siren shoves the images in the bastard's face letting him know that even though the justice system let these poor children down, the Daughters of Doom have every intention of making him pay for his crimes; for the lives he has ruined.

"You sick fuck!" Siren yells, spit flying from her mouth in a fit of rage. "Look at them," she screams, crammin the last three pictures of three small bodies into his face, the ones we found on this sick pervert's home property. "Ava Turner, Michael Homes, and Asia Westly. These poor babies were found buried in your fucking yard!"

The portly man's sweat rolls down his face mixing with the blood from where we've been cutting and punching him, making his torture slow and sweet.

I laugh at seeing the fear glint in his widened pupils and the way he backs up as much as he physically can away from Siren. "Do you know what we do to child fuckers?" I say coolily, holding my knife to his throat. The sharp edge nicks his skin causing a warm puddle to form around my feet. There's a darkened spot on his crotch where he pissed himself.

"Oh fuck no, Davenport. You're not getting off with a sliced throat. Nope, you're not getting off that easy." I put on a pair of white latex gloves and unbutton his pants, shoving them down to his ankles. The man's tiny, flaccid penis nearly shrinks, turtling inside his balls.

"Oh! Look ladies!" I blurt out, pointing at the man's small dick. "No wonder he can't find a woman his age, he has a micro-peen."

Pushing down on his shriveled junk, I pull his appendage out of hiding and use my blade to cut it off. He howls like a wounded animal in pain that's nothing more than a mumble thanks to the gag covering his mouth. A crimson fountain quickly gushes from his crotch, coating the floor in a puddle of the pedophile's blood and urine.

"Siren, finish Mr. Davenport off. Quinn, do what you do best and make sure this slime ball is never found," I order, taking off the gloves and throwing them at the blubbering bastard's face that is quickly losing its color by the minute. "Everyone else meet back at the clubhouse."

Quinn is the cleaner, also known as the GrimReaper. She's the person who cleans up bodies, removes DNA and makes sure there is no evidence to point to us. She has a special formula that melts bodies down to nothing but sludge, kind of like a candle melting. She's small but strong like nitroglycerin. They say dynamite comes in small packages. That's exactly what she is and besides that; the bitch loves to clean. Our clubhouse stays spotless thanks to her.

Another one down, many more to go, I think as I climb onto my bike and head back to the clubhouse, back to the place I call home.

Being President of an MC is hard, and being a President for the *only* female motorcycle club is hell. No one takes females seriously. They expect us to be sweet and spread our legs. That's about all anyone expects from us, but we are much, much more than that.

As President of the Daughters of Doom Motorcycle Club, I have strong counsel members that precede me. All the ladies included in the Daughters of Doom Motorcycle Club, fifteen in total with the three prospects, we are all survivors of one situation or another. Some were prostitutes, sex slaves, club girls, runaways, abused and homeless. All from different walks of life, but we come together in the best way to help one another.

We created a safe environment and sisterhood where we are family. Sisters. Not by blood, but by our choosing and we all provide and take care of each other. Most of us are single, a few with children and men are a rare entity inside the confines of our clubhouse unless accompanied by a member, except Micah. Micah is what some consider our house boy. He cooks and cleans and looks after the needs of the ladies. I'm sure sexually for some, but mostly if we need something done like laundry and we are busy, he will do it for us. I adore Micah, but have never been sexually involved with him. I guess if this were a men's motorcycle club, and if Micah was female you would consider him a clubwhore. He gets free rent, food and most everything else he needs; and the fucker is loyal and trustworthy. That's what matters. We are like any other family, we fuss, argue, and end up making up after a few punches and everything is okay again.

We own legit businesses too. The Kitty Kat Klub is a strip joint owned and operated by the MC It hosts both male and female dancers. All are legal, all are age appropriate and all receive frequent drug tests. We even test the workers regularly for sexually transmitted diseases even though prostitution isn't allowed in the club and the worker will be fired if caught selling sexual favors.

We own two marijuana dispensaries which are also lawfully legit with special weed grown in house by Indica. Indica knows weed like a philosopher knows Aristotle. Her special grown herbs go from a lil bit fucked up to seeing dragons and shit. She's the best of the best when it comes to Mary Jane. Even though at times you would think she's whacked out of her brain when you catch her singing and talking to the plants, or even sleeping alongside them like her own little herb babies, she's not. If you ever got a chance to taste her cannabis, you'd feel as if she were cuddling you and cooing a lullaby in your ear while your eyes got heavy. Her shit is that good.

We own a few diners, a garage and a metaphysical shop. You will not believe how many people are into the paranormal these days. All of these businesses are strictly legal as well. Members of the club run the businesses and of course are paid for their work, like normal jobs.

We even own a funeral home as well that has a convenient crematorium. Which is another way to get rid of loose ends and DNA. These businesses are in an organization's name that cannot be tracked back to the club or any member involved. Sneaky bitches, aren't we?

Now illegally, we don't have anything to do with sex slavery or prostitution, no skin trade whatsoever, like I said some of my sisters are survivors of it, but guns are a different story. Do we sell those to thugs, other bike clubs, or people on the street? Fuck, no. We are the guns for hire. That's right, hit women. We take case by case depending on the situation, what the person has done and whether or not the counsel agrees that death is needed. If death isn't the answer, we ruin them in other ways like public humiliation, breaking their bank accounts, or beat downs. We decide the punishment and what fits the crimes which are voted on during church.

Death is gifted upon those who have killed the innocent, child molesters, murderers, rapists and pedophiles. We are clean, efficient and get the job done with no ties back to us. People rarely think that women are monsters; or that we enjoy killing. I can say that isn't the case when it comes to us. The lives we take are menaces to society. They are less than human and as far as I care, it doesn't bother me a bit to kill them. I think of it as taking the garbage out and getting paid extremely well to do it.

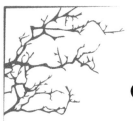

Chapter 4: Ace

Now Twenty-nine years old

"God, Mur you're giving me a fucking headache," I say, rubbing my temples. "The drop isn't that fucking hard. You and Price meet with Glade and his right hand, get the money, give them the weed and jet." I throw my boots up on the table making a clunk.

"Okay, Prez. Don't get your panties in a bunch. We're leaving now," Murphy, my Vice President says, as he starts to get up from his seat.

Murphy, my best friend and the club VP grew up with me, around the club. His father was the Vice President of the club when my father was President. We prospected together and were patched in on the same day. Murphy is a big son of a bitch, a monstrous force and always down to get his hands dirty; if necessary. He understands more than most what it means to wear the patch. Once a crow, always a crow; unless you are dead. He has always stood with me when I've changed rules to better the club and has never let the club or me down. The only problem with Murphy, besides his anger issues, is his need to fuck anything with a pussy.

"Oh, Mur?" I call, giving him a scowl as I plant my feet on the ground and lean forward in my seat. "You ever talk to me again like that and I'll break your fucking jaw."

He turns around, looking me in the eye. His shoulders sag with defeat.. "I'm sorry, Ace. Just been a rough day."

"Be safe brother." I nod, giving him permission to leave the war room.

Being a motorcycle club member is hard, but being the President of a one percenter club is fucking hell. My brothers by choice will always have my back, and I'll have theirs, but some decisions I have to make to keep the club and my brothers safe and those can be unyielding. I hold the lives of the members in my hands. I'm responsible for the things that happen because my father was the president. When he had his tragic accident, I was left in the position of President.

I'm not saying my father was a shitty president, but my father was a shitty *fucking* president. Not in his younger days, but as he got older he was definitely rotten. Things like money missing from the books, abuse of club girls, ol' ladies, dealings with other clubs going south, all things that made him not up to par. I've been trying to fix as much as I can and dealing with other clubs to bridge the gaps and help each other out. Instead of measuring dick sizes and trying to take over each other's territory. When dad died a year ago, his counsel members decided to retire their positions as well and I appointed my friend Murphy as Vice president, Zeus as Enforcer, and Bones as our Grim Reaper. Price and Cash were voted in by the other counsel members.

I was born into the Crows, and my whole life has been involved with them in one way or another. I am a hard but fair president and do what I can to help and to protect my brothers. My chosen family. We don't fuck with the skin trade, we don't sell hardcore drugs or guns we are mostly legal now besides the weed, because it's not legal here yet.

I sit back in my chair, replacing my shitkickers on the tabletop and take a swig of Jack straight from the bottle. After throwing four Advil in my mouth, I take another long pull of the warm caramel, oak Tennessee Whiskey.

"Fucking headaches," I murmur, to myself as my cell rings.

"This is Olivia Youngstown of River, Daniels, and Peter's attorneys at law. We have this number as an emergency Contact for Mrs. Katherine Weatherspoon." A proverbial bucket of cold water is dumped on my head. My face drops as I massage the back of my neck. *Fuck.* I haven't heard that name in years.

"Uh. I know her. I don't know how my number got to be her emergency contact. I haven't seen or heard from her in over ten years," I inform the person on the other end of the line, sitting up straighter in my chair.

"Well I'm not sure either, but I wanted to inform you that she has passed on and that she has a will leaving some things to the Murder of Crows Motorcycle Club and to a daughter by the name of, Kelsey Weatherspoon. We haven't been able to verify the daughter's whereabouts and we're wondering if you know how to contact Ms. Weatherspoon?" My heart starts beating out of my chest like a bull ramming against my ribs. I haven't heard anyone mention Kelsey's name for a long goddamn time and now they can't *find* her.

"I'll see what I can do about locating her, but I make no promises. Maybe, give me the number to your office and I'll let you know what I find out." I scrawl out the lawyer's number and press the end button on my phone.

Kelsey. Fucking Kelsey. The one who got away. The one that just fucking left me without saying a word. Her mother is dead and she's nowhere to be found. The thoughts in my mind take me to that summer when I taught her how to ride. God, I loved that girl even then. Her mother was always gone, leaving Kelsey to fend for herself. They barely even had food. Kelsey pretty much raised herself.

Wanting to let them know what has happened, I notify my counselors with a quick message telling them to join me in the war room again. A few will remember Kat but most of us are around the same age as Kelsey, and none of them will remember her like I do.

Chapter 5: Kelsey

Then Twelve years old

"What a beauty," I say, looking at the nine millimeter pistol Talon got from his dad for his birthday. The butterflies flutter in my belly filling me with excitement. "You're gonna teach me to shoot aren't ya?"

Talon gazes at me suspiciously with one eyebrow raised. "Are you going to shoot me, pretty girl?"

"No, silly. I'd never hurt you," I answer. My neck and cheeks heat with what I've heard him call me, blushing. "I like when you teach me things. You already taught me how to ride, fight, how to dis-arm a knife attacker, and self-defense, now it's time to teach me how to shoot!" I say, taking Talon's hand into mine. "You've taught me how to take care of myself and a girl needs to know this stuff." I lean up on my tippy toes and kiss him on the cheek. Maybe that will help change his mind.

He pulls me closer to him, my back to his front, the gun in my right hand. "See this here? This is safety. Make sure this is on at all times unless you're going to shoot." He turns the gun to the side, showing me the button and moving it to the safety position. "Don't point at anything you're not planning on shooting either."

With his hand in mine, he shows me how to hold the gun. His arms wrap around me and his warm breath tickles my ear when he says, "Okay, now take the safety off Kels, and hold the gun like I showed you. I want you to aim at that soda can and press the trigger, okay?"

"Okay," I reply, taking a deep breath.

I hold out the nine millimeter, check the safety, line it up, aim at the can and pull the trigger. There's a loud pop and the can falls off the makeshift bench we were sitting on just moments before. I place the safety back on like Talon taught me and hand it back to him, so I can check out the damage of the can.

"Look, Talon!" I squeal, excitedly. "I'm a pro!" I laugh, holding up the can to show him the hole I made proudly.

"You're a natural, Kid," he says, looking at the can. "Better than my first shot."

"Don't call me kid," I retort, crossing my arms across my chest. "I'm only two years younger than you!"

"I'm sorry my ol' lady," he replies, in a joking tone. "Forgive me?"

"I'm going to marry you one day," I say, snarling at him and slapping him on the arm. "But, you cannot call me your ol' lady."

We practiced a lot more that year. He would bring more guns to show me and I would beg him to teach me to shoot them all. I was a pretty good shot for a twelve year old and his eyes gleamed with a sense of pride every time I hit a target. The best thing though, every time I had a good hit, I was rewarded with a kiss on the cheek, so each time I made sure to hit the bulls eye.

Chapter 6: Talon

Then fourteen years old

Kelsey's big, brown, chocolate eyes stare up at me every time she hits the target. She is so damn adorable. Her excitement is contagious and we celebrate with every can that's taken down. Her dark hair blows in the wind, whafting the scent of orange creamsicle push pops in my face. I inhale deeply, commemorating this moment to memory and I peer down at her glowing face. I know she's worth all the shit I get from my friends for hanging out with a girl younger than me. They just don't know her like I do.

She's mature for her age. Hell, she's more mature than me at times. Even when I know her mom leaves her to survive on her own, her head is still held high when I would be lost if I was put in her shoes. I admire her excitement over learning new things, the smile that lights her face when she masters a new skill, and the way she takes shit from no one makes her a total badass with hell of a right hook.

Anytime, I get a new weapon or learn a new fight move or defensive maneuver I teach it to her. We still have to hide from my dad, but it is well worth it. The days I get to spend with Kelsey. They're the best days of my life. We've moved up from the play fighting we did two years ago. Nowadays we hug, hold hands, and I give her kisses on the cheek, but that's as far as we have gone. It's all pretty innocent compared to what my friends have said they've done with their girlfriends. The twins Price and Cash and I know Murphy has all had sex with girls, sometimes even the girls at the club will fuck around and give them blowjobs, hoping that when they are old enough they will let them be their Crowettes. I know though, as soon as she turns seventeen, I am going to ask her to be mine, and I have no doubt she'll say yes.

Chapter 7: Storm

Now

"Okay. I'll leave tomorrow. Thank you for letting me know." I end the conversation and slump over in my chair.

My mother is dead. I can't believe it. I haven't talked to her since the night of my seventeenth birthday. An overdose is what they claimed her cause of death was from. That doesn't surprise me though considering she used to buy drugs with our grocery money. I have to act like I wasn't hungry when I'd hang out with Talon. He'd thankfully share his snacks with me anyways. Deep down I think he knew, he was just nice enough to never bring it up. I shake my head to clear my thoughts.

"You okay, Madam President?" Chyna, my vice president asks.

She's smart, strong and always has my back. Her road name suits her. She's named after the woman wrestler, who's muscular and tall. Of course, on top of all that, she also looks like a china doll. Except she isn't fragile, no not breakable or dainty, but she is broken. Hell, all of us are in our own ways. Chyna is a badass jiu jitsu black belt and a woman's body building champion. She's tough as nails. I once saw her take on three big ass muscular dudes and not shed a drop of sweat.

"Hey, I asked if you were okay?" she asks again this time with more worry in her tone as she saunters into the war room. It's a big room in the center of the club house with a massive table where we hold our meetings called church.

"Uh, yeah," I reply after shaking away some of the memories from my past and coming back to reality. Chyna looks at me over with her brows bunched in concern. I turn and take a beer out of the small refrigerator in the corner, knowing I'll need this. "Message the counsel. I need to talk to y'all please," I say, taking a guzzle of my beer.

Ten minutes later, the war room is filled with all of my council members. I scan the room filled with the girls, ney, the women in front of me. All of them are different sizes, from different backgrounds, different personalities. All of them would give their life for another person in the room. Sisterhood, built stronger than any blood connection. Family of our own choosing. They're all chatting among themselves, some are laughing and their faces glow until I find them. My posture becomes straighter as my chest fills with pride. I'm proud of the sisterhood I brought together.

I clear my throat to gain their attention and I'm not sure exactly how I should feel at this time about the information I'm about to share with them. All the same, I can't keep anything from them. They all look to me for instruction, waiting to hear what I have to say.

"My mom died last week," I say, in a matter-of-fact voice that's void of any emotions. "I need Siren, Chyna and Trinity to get packed. Y'all are coming with me."

"Trinity, you need to get us to my hometown, Jackson, Kentucky. Make sure you contact all of the clubs along the way. It doesn't matter if they give you shit because we are women, this is a courtesy call," I command, standing up and spreading my palms over the old oak table. My fingers brush the edge of the brand that symbolizes all that I've worked so hard for. "Besides the Murder of Crows MC, those I'll inform personally."

Trinity is a femme fatale. She has the body and face of a runway model. She's beautiful with blonde hair and blue eyes. You can't look at her and tell that she's a tough biker bitch that will stab you, cut you from sternum to belly button and not think twice about it. However, as hot as her blade wielding is, her love for traveling and road management is greater. That's what she is to the Daughter of Doom, the road captain. She finds quick routes, stops, and things for club trips.

Trinity also makes sure maintenance and provisions are up to par with all the bikes. Her girlfriend, Katana, helps her in the garage from time to time.

"Bear and Quinn, you two are in charge while we are away. Shouldn't be more than a few days." I grab another beer from the refrigerator and kill it.

"Yes, boss," they both say unanimously.

"Text me if you have any problems or concerns." My focus is on the group but my words are directed at my right two hand women. "Okay, get your shit together and make sure you're packing heat."

The girls get up and leave the room, and I think about my mother and the fucking hell we are about to walk into.

Thanks mom. I think, sarcastically.

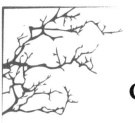

Chapter 8: Ace

Now

I call the lawyers office, while fighting with myself on whether I should have or not. I want to see Kelsey, but not at the expense of her mother dying. I've wondered through the years where she was, if she was happy, and why she left so suddenly. How could she leave me so easily? I've had private detectives, used Techie's extraordinary skills, and it's like she disappeared from the planet. My eighteen year old heart was broken when I realized she had left and didn't even tell me goodbye. She left me confused, sad, and heart broken. I tried through many women to get over Kelsey, sinking my cock into nameless, faceless pussy to try to ease my broken heart. Now she's coming back to town and I have every intention of asking her every question I've wanted to know the answers to for the last decade.

A hard pounding comes at my bedroom door just after I get out of the shower. I throw a blue towel around me as steam continues to billow out into my room. "What the fuck do you want?" I ask, yanking the door open.

A girl with long blonde hair stands in the entryway, wearing nothing but a lace bra and a pair of thongs. Her round shiny blue eyes peer up at me as if she's a lost fawn that's been sent straight into the lion's den.

"Hi, Prez, the boys sent me up here. Said you might want some company tonight." Her voice is high, squeaky, almost child-like.

I glare at her with a scowl on my face. "No, Ginger, I don't need any company. Go hit up Bull or Rooster. I'm sure they will be more than willing for your company tonight." Uninterested in her offer, I close the door in her face.

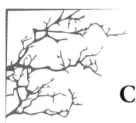

Chapter 9: Kelsey

Seventeen years old

I smooth my baby hairs down with nervous energy and gaze at myself in the mirror. My dark blue dress conforming to my curves just right before cascading down to just above my knees. My cleavage can be seen but it's not showing in a "slutty" way, only showing the top of my chest. It's the right amount of exceptionally classy with just a smidge of trashy. Besides the fine vellus around my face that doesn't want to stay down, my hair is perfect. It's curled in long ringlets like shavings of chocolate that lay against my back. Even my makeup makes me appear as if I'm graced to this earth as an angel to walk amongst mere mortals. It's light with eyeliner and mascara and my lips are a pretty light pink. If everything is as it should be, then why am I so nervous?

Because tonight is the night Talon is claiming me as his "Crone" in front of the whole club on my seventeenth birthday. I'm elated, and cannot wait to officially be Talon's girl. His ol 'lady and when I get eighteen, I'll happily wear his property patch, but I can't deny that edge of nervous energy that seems to invade every free space in my body. *It's going to be fine. It's going to be fine. You look great.* I repeat affirmation in my head as my hands rest on the vanity. My fingers brush the bottle of perfume. Ah, maybe that's what I'm missing. I spray a few spritzes of body spray and take a few twirls in my dress, capturing the falling mist in the air. That should do it.

I jump in my mom's beat up seventy-nine BMW The door screeching as I pull it closed and sit, staring off into the woods. After taking a few deep breaths, I start the engine and head to the clubhouse.

Once I arrive at the old brick building at just after eight, the music is already loud, and there is a shit ton of motorcycles out front. The only one I don't see is Talon's bike. It must be in the garage or something. I run my clammy palms over my bare thighs, gathering my courage. This is a woman's big day, it's normal to be a little nervous, right?

Without further stalling, I head on into the clubhouse. Weed, liquor, and sex invades my nostrils, tickling the back of my throat. I gag at the air pollution that slaps me in my face. I recover quickly and scan the room for Talon, but I cannot find him anywhere. Where is he?

"Happy birthday, babygirl," Jaxx, one of the brothers whispers in my ear, wrapping his arm around me from behind.

"Thanks. Where's Talon?" I ask, taking a step away from him. He smells like chewing tobacco and body odor.

"Prez had him running an errand really quick, he should be back anytime." He steps closer to me, again. "Let's go get a drink for the birthday girl." He grabs my hand and drags me toward the bar. My stomach churns with disgust and I yank my hand away.

"Just a coke for me, please."

"No, no, no give her a Jack and Coke, Prospect." Jaxx winks at the biker in training and says, "it's her birthday."

The prospect slides me a glass and I take a sip. The liquor burns my throat as it goes down. I'm not used to drinking but I'm pretty sure this is more Jack than it is Coke.

"Thanks," I say, taking the tumbler from the bartop and over walking to a chair in a corner.

I plop down in the seat and pull out my phone to call Talon. His voicemail isn't set up and he isn't answering. *Come on, Talon.*

My glass sweats creating a puddle on the table. I run my finger through it, writing out Talon's name. I'm not sure how much time passes, but I continue drinking Jack and Coke to dull my senses. The aroma of this place has my stomach twisting into knots. The drawing on the table blurs and I think I might be crying. I rub my eyes but the distortion of my vision continues. A dizzy feeling hits me, my head begins swimming. *I feel off. Something's not right. Did I drink too much?*

If I could just go to the bathroom and splash some water on my face, I'll feel much better. I climb out of my chair and nearly topple to the floor. My legs are heavy and my focus is hazy. I'm having a hard time walking since my feet are numb and I try to drag them along the floor. Thankfully there's a brick structure already in place to guide me where I need to go. The wall. That's it. That's what helps to hold me up, but the world around me spins. I'm being tugged the opposite direction by someone. The smell of him is so strong that I double over.

"Where are you going, birthday girl? The party is just about to start!" Jaxx throws me over his shoulder like I am a sack of potatoes.

My head swings back and forth along with my arms that dangle over my head. The floor races by as if I'm sitting in the back seat of a car. How the scenery rushes by in a blur of brown and green, but this view is missing that bright emerald cheer. No, the dark mahogany floors are missing all their shine from this devastating place.

His shoes pound with every step and I can hear it in my head. *Boom. Boom. BOOM.* It's in sync with my pulse and the blood rushing in my ears. He throws me on something hard. I try telling him to stop, but my voice is lost in my throat. I try to fight him, punch and kick, but I can't move my arms or legs. I try to scream, but no words will come out of my mouth. I can't even cry. My body is useless and there is nothing I can do but succumb to the blackness that is enveloping me.

I wake up off and on as different guys plow into me. Their nasty sweaty bodies drip onto my skin. I want this to stop. I want to scrub the flesh on my bones raw to rid this memory of them. My mind is fighting them, but my body is betraying me. My mouth is dry and my voice box won't work. The thought of ending all of them as I see the guys climb on top of me and do what they want to me is the only thing that's keeping air moving through my lungs. I try to scream over and over wanting Talon to save me, to help me from his club, but all I see are faces. I keep cataloging them as I go to the void and back again.

But Talon isn't coming and all I have is myself.

I JOLT UP. PAIN WRACKING every inch of my body. My legs are hurting, and my body feels like I've been hit by a car. I hold my head as if at any moment it will bust and split in two. With the tips of my fingers, I rub circles on my temples until the stabbing dulls to a low throb and am able to move my legs to the side of the pool table. There are hand shaped bruises all over my legs and I begin inspecting myself further. The green felt is dark and I look down at the pain between my thighs where I see smeared blood. There are cuts and bruises on my abdomen, stomach and my thighs. I choke down the vomit that arises and look away. I can't even look at myself. Tears prick my eyes and I shove that emotion down deep into a box of my own making. There's no time to feel sorry for myself.

My arms and legs are heavy, still hard for me to move and my heart is hammering against my ribcage as though it's going to burst. I try to get enough saliva in my mouth to wet it, but it's not happening. My mouth is parched to the point my tongue is made of cotton balls. *Water.* I need water.

I crawl off the pool table and as soon as I stand, pain shoots through my legs. My knees buckle and I grab hold of the chair in front of me. I'm wobbly like I'm drunk. The pressure in my head still causes my vision to blur. I throw my dress back on that I find thrown on the floor and search around for my panties which I can't find. *Sonofabitch must've kept them as a trophy.*

With my shoes in hand, I examine the room, searching for an exit I can slip out of and when I find it, I run. I'm like a new baby fawn as I stumble multiple times, but I finally push open the metal door. The sky is dark, starless even. I look up anyways wishing on the invisible night to take me away from this place. The air kisses my heated cheeks like a soothing balm to my soul. *I can do this.*

The gravel bites into my heels as I try to find my car, but it isn't where I left it. I have to leave quickly. My breathing is labored as I run, searching the few bikes out front. I'm stuck here. *I'm stuck.* I pull the strands of my hair and slow my panicked inhales and notice that one of the members left the keys in ignition. That's it. My heart soars. I look up at the empty sky, giving it a silent thank you before I hop on the motorcycle and take off heading to my mommy.

The bike beneath me slides on the bends in the road and I'm not even sure how I make it to my house. Maybe it was the adrenaline rush of trying to get out of there or maybe it was the night sky that held me together. I'm not sure, but once I pull into the overgrown grass in front of the trailer. My car just happens to be in the driveway, where I didn't park it. *Those fucking assholes.* What were they planning on doing with me, if I hadn't woken up when I did?

I lose what little control I have left. The bike, still running, falls to its side as I hop off on shaking legs. The handle sinking into the soft ground.

I got this. I just need my mommy.

With a trembling hand, I push open the unlocked flimsy door to the trailer. My feet crunch on old burger wrappers and knock over abandoned half full beer bottles. The mess is of no concern to me right now. I'll clean it up later. My focus is getting to my mommy and I find her where she always is when she's not at the clubhouse. The old tan couch that we got off the side of the road a few years ago sinks in where she sits drinking a bottle of Jack and smoking a cigarette. The ashes sag on the half burned cancer stick, ready to fall at any moment.

"Mom, please help me," I cry, as I stagger into the living room. My eyes are full of tears and my body aches all over. "I went to my party at the clubhouse and they drugged and raped me." The words come out as fragile as glass that's ready to break.

"What did you expect, Kelsey?" she says, wrinkling her nose up at me. "You went there looking like a whore. Look at that dress, that slutty makeup. They treated you like they treat me. They just wanted to welcome you like they do all the Crowettes." The distaste for me rolls off her with a well practiced sneer before chugging her fifth of whiskey.

"You're just gonna drink and blame me when I tell you I was raped by no telling how many men?" I motion to my chest with a splayed hand willing her to see me as I hold back the whence of pain in my side.

"Get over it, Kelsey. Ain't nothing you can do about it. The Crows practically own this fucking town." She snubs her cigarette, extinguishing the flame.

My brows pull together and my mouth falls open. This is it. The one time I expected her to care about me or anything that happens to me, but again I'm left disappointed. Even if she was never there for me any other time I needed her, this was the moment I could have forgiven her. My heart sinks down to my feet and my eyes burn with unshed tears that I refuse to let fall.

"Fuck you, you old whore. I hope those bikers make you happy."

I clench my fists at my side and limp to my bedroom to throw what little belongings I have in a bag. This place is rotten to the core. I have to get away from her, from this house, from this fucking town. Once I have all my belongings, I grab the picture of Talon and me by our tree and sling it in the bag. I don't know if he was a part of this or not, but I can't go back to the clubhouse. The only person I have to save me is myself, because as far as I'm concerned there is nothing left for me in this town.

"You'll be back."

"We'll see about that." I glare at my mother one last time. The door slams hard enough to make it fall off the hinge as I make my way out into the night.

EVERYTHING IS WHITE, almost virginal, but I know it's a fabrication due to the strong chemical smells. Bleach, antiseptics, and *human shit*. This normally wouldn't bother me since it's to be expected in a place like this, but my nerves are fired and I'm irritated as I go to the emergency room admittance window and lie.

The story I tell them is that I went to a party and I was raped and possibly drugged, but that I didn't know by who or how many, so a half-lie anyway. They take me back, perform a rape kit before doing a small procedure and checking over the rest of my body. They even do an x-ray, because I think one of them beat me while I was unconscious. They tell me the tests may take hours to come back, so I push the plastic covered pillow under my head and curl up on my side. I try to rest up, because I'm sneaking out as soon as I get the results of all the tests. I just want to see what all is wrong with me, then out of this shit-hole town.

"Ms.Weatherspoon, incase you didn't know when we do a rape kit, we take DNA samples." Her eyes shine with pity that I didn't ask for. "I am sorry to inform you that we found five different DNA strains." She pauses, allowing that information to sink in. "You also have a cracked rib and some bruises but that should heal in a few days along with the small tear to your inner labia we had to stitch up. Those should dissolve in a few days as well." She hands me a plastic cup with two pills and a glass of water. "Pain medication." I take it from her hands, slinging the contents into my mouth. Anything will help take the edge off right now. The doctor waits for me to gulp down every last drop before adding, "It is up to you whether you want it, but we can also provide you with a Plan B pill. It's usually referred to as the morning after which you can also find them at most pharmacies if you decide to think about it."

"Yes," I blurt out. My mind was already made up before the pill option was ever provided. I won't let those bastards control my life.

The nurse gives me a curt nod before handing me another small cup with a small blue pill inside it. "There are officers here that want to talk to you," she says, glancing toward the emergency room doors.

"Can I use the restroom first?"

"Sure, honey. I'll tell them to wait."

When the nurse walks out, I snatch up my clothes and shoes before heading to the bathroom. I take off the hospital gown and put on the disheveled dress. The one I was wearing when I arrived at the party, and the only thing left as a reminder of this awful day. I sneak past the nurses station and the cops that are more focused on the hospital coffee than their actual jobs. My BMW—that's used, rode hard and beat up like me—sits in the front row. I jump in and turn the key. The fields on both sides of the road, whoosh by as I head out of Kentucky. The small town I grew up in grows even smaller in my rearview and without looking back, I hold up my middle finger to the backseat.

Chapter 10: Talon

Then... 18 years old

F*ucking, Prez. Fucking, Dad.* I think, jumping on my bike. He fucking knew I wanted to be here at the club when Kelsey arrived for her birthday party. I'm going to claim her in front of everyone, so they know she's mine. She's my girl. She always has been, but I want the club to know it too. I was going to call her, but my cellphone is missing. Now, I'm in bum-fucked Beattyville meeting with a guy who sells dime bags. He's not even the normal fucker we mess with. I know something isn't right and I feel it in my gut. As soon as I make the deal, I race back to the clubhouse.

The gravel lot crunches beneath my tires and it's filled with the other member's bikes, but Kel's vehicle is nowhere in sight. Is this the foreboding I was sensing? That she backed out and changed her mind?

When I push open the door to the clubhouse, dad is already there with his hand for the money. Now that that's taken care of, I saddle up to the bar and ask if anyone has seen Kelsey. I get a few weird looks, but no one claims they have seen her. My shoulders sag with despair at the thought that maybe she didn't show up because she doesn't want me anymore. This is her way of saying she isn't ready to be claimed. I knew growing up she wanted nothing to do with the club, but I held out hope that maybe she would do it for me. I get me a beer from the bar and chug it and wait a few more minutes to see if she shows up.

There's not even a moment of peace, because I have to fight off a couple Crowettes, the clubwhores that are always trying to get a brother to patch them as their ol' ladies. It doesn't matter if you are on the council or not but they rather you were, and since I'm the President's son all the Crowettes try sinking their talons in me. They kiss on my neck and run their nails over my chest. Their suggestive notions cause a shiver to run down my spine and not in a good way. I shake them off and go outside for some air.

It's almost one in the morning. The sky's the bleakest I've ever seen or maybe it's because I haven't actually taken the time to look at it much these days. That nagging sensation pulls at the edges of my mind, pulling me toward my bike. There's no way Kels would have not shown up. There has to be a reason and I need to see her. The desire to go to Kelsey's to see why is overwhelming. I hop on my bike and spray rocks as I speed out of the lot.

I'm a bit buzzed, but the wind in my face and the thrill of the ride helps to ground me. It's not long before I'm banging on the door of her trailer. It's been knocked off its hinges and I get no answer, so I pull it open to find Kelsey's mother naked on the couch passed out.

"Kelsey!" I call, making my way through the little house until I get to her bedroom. That eerie wave washes over me harder this time and I suck in a sharp breath. All her things are *gone*.

"She's not here, Talon," Mrs. Witherspoon says, as I walk back to the living room. She laughs, sitting up not even caring that she's on full display. "She went to the clubhouse and you weren't there so she fucked a bunch of your brothers and came here to tell me she was leaving and not coming back." She leans back with a mischievous smirk and inserts a cancer stick between her chapped lips. "If you're looking for a lay though." She spreads her legs further apart, putting on a show before lighting the cigarette. "You're always welcome in my bed." She blows out a cloud of smoke in my direction.

Fire courses through my veins and I clench my fists at my side. "You're *fucking* lying," I accuse. "You're nothing but a lying, drunk, addicted club whore. Kelsey loves me. She would never leave me without saying a word."

Mrs. Witherspoon takes a drink of the almost empty bottle of booze in front of her and shrugs. "Suit yourself."

I walk out the door not bothering to close it and jump on my Harley. Pain radiates through my chest and I grit my teeth to hold onto that anger. My heart's broken, but I can't let anyone see me weak. Everyone said she didn't show up at the clubhouse. *Was her mother lying? Did she fuck guys at the clubhouse? Where the fuck is she?*

That bitch was lying, I know she was. So was everyone at the clubhouse. Something happened tonight. They did something to my girl, and I won't stop until I find her. I'll search for her every day of my life. Kelsey Witherspoon is mine and I'll have her beside me one way or another.

Chapter 11: Storm

Now

I put on my leather cut with the Daughter of Doom Motorcycle Club written in big purple letters across my shoulder blades and the shield in the middle of my back. My hair covers it most of the time unless I'm in business then I pull it up in a ponytail for all to see. Especially when I want them to remember who they are dealing with. On the breast pocket is my name adorned with a crown and the President patch is beneath it on the right side.

I love wearing my cut, and how it makes me feel wearing it, almost like I am free. When I'm without it, I feel naked. Even more so than I am without my weapons which I strap on next. I put my serrated hunting knife in its sheath at my thigh, a smaller one in my boot, and another one in the pocket of my cut. You never know what problems you will run into on road trips, so I check my twenty-two caliber, and my nine millimeter and grab ammo for them. I also grab my Lapara, a sawed off shotgun which I named Janette. Once my stuff is packed and I'm heavily armed, I send out a message to the group, ready to hit the road on my jacked up Harley.

My girl.

The love of my life.

My bike.

I have a strong passion for riding. We all do or we wouldn't be a motorcycle club. I've loved riding since the first time I climbed behind Talon. The wind in my face, the feeling of peace, the power between my legs, there is nothing fucking like It. Riding a motorcycle is better than chocolate, better than a cold beer on a hot day. Fuck, it's even better than sex, well better than any sex I've ever had.

We hit the road ten minutes later heading towards the Appalachian Mountains, towards the place where I used to call home, towards hell. *Kentucky, fucking Kentucky.* Where all my nightmares come from.

IT'S NOT EVEN DAYLIGHT—WHICH seems fitting since that's when I left that god forsaken place to begin with—when we start our two and a half thousand mile journey across the states from Heron, California to the small Appalachian town of Jackson, Kentucky. Trinity, like the brilliant road manager she is, has our schedule down to minutes for every stop, bathroom breaks, meals, and hotels for the night.

The weather goes from an eighty-five degrees dry heat to a sixty-five degrees wet as we make our way into the mountains of Eastern Kentucky. We make it to my mother's house in three and a half days.

The house is a disgrace, as if it has been abandoned for years instead of being uninhabited ten days ago. I turn off my bike and gaze upon the home of my childhood. The white paint is chipping away exposing the previous color that's been hiding underneath. The front door is off from its hinges which was probably never fixed from where I slammed it years ago, and a window where my bedroom used to be has a cardboard box taped over it where someone must've busted it out. This place looks like where hope comes to die. I know mine did.

"This is where you grew up?" Siren looks at me like I am growing two heads. "It smells like hopelessness and regret lives here. I believe there is something dead in this overgrown yard."

"It looks like a haunted attraction," Trinity says, examining a spider web that is hanging in the corner of one of the windows.

"Yeah, it's the star of my nightmares. It definitely still haunts the fuck out of me."

We sit idled amongst the tall grass, staring at the house as if we're expecting a ghost or monster to appear. I let out a sigh as I climb off my Harley. My knees knock together and weakness takes over. I have to grab my bike quickly in order to keep from falling. Am I ready for this trip down memory lane? Yes, I can do this. I recover and saunter up to the house of horrors and reach above the door to a small ledge where my mom always kept a spare key. The girl's follow me, keeping their thoughts to themselves. It's a heavy weight on my shoulders as I'm forced to revisit the skeleton's of my past and they know I need this moment of silence.

I fumble the key into the lock. The broken screen door bangs against the trailer as it flaps in the wind. I open the door revealing the same rooms I left so many years ago. The house looks exactly the same as if left just yesterday and not ten years ago. A brown wooden couch from the 80's, an ugly coffee table stained with glass rings and a half of a bottle of whiskey on it and a thirty-year-old green reclining chair sits in the living room . There's also a rocking chair and an old box television set that looks like it's traveling back in time. The odor of tobacco, stale liquor, weed, and mildew pollute the air. I can still picture my mother sitting on that ugly sofa drinking like a god damned fish. The smoke from her cigarette engulfing her like she was some kind of evil Djinn and I hear the last words she ever spoke to me, *You'll be back.*

She was right about one thing, I guess. I did come back but not until she was buried six feet deep and unable to see me now. She doesn't deserve the me I am today. That's for damn sure.

As I make my way through the house of hell with my top lip curled in disgust, I know damn well I have no interest in this house or anything in it. My phone flashes with a text from Quinn, pulling me away from my current thoughts.

Quinn: Y'all okay boss? I haven't heard from ya since yesterday.

Me: Yeah. We are. Everything going well at HQ?

Quinn: The prospects got a little mouthy after I made them help Micah scrub the clubhouse, but we shut them up quickly.

Me: Good. Everything is okay here. Keep them busy. Thanks for the check up.

Quinn: NP. Prez. Talk later.

I shove my phone into my pocket and trudge back into the living room, where three sets of eyes are looking at me.

"There's nothing here that I'm interested in. If you see something that tickles your fancy, have at it," I say, sitting on the old couch and the others take it as a sign for them to do the same.

I pick up the whiskey bottle from the table sitting before me and wipe the mouth of the bottle before taking a nice long chug. The whiskey burns my throat as I drink it and the fire burns down to my belly. It's been a long time since I've drank anything stronger than a beer. I've always been hell bent and determined not to end up like my mother. The memories must be getting to me harder than I thought.

"No offense, Madam Prez," Chyna chimes in, wrinkling her nose. "I don't think anything here is my cup of tea either." She grabs the bottle from my hand and takes a swig. "Except for maybe this," she adds, before taking another drink before passing it to Siren. Her big body is squeezed into the old rocking chair, reminding me of an adult trying to sit in a toddler chair and it takes everything in me not to laugh.

"NONE TAKEN." I WAVE off any worries. "This place hasn't changed in over ten years." I nod towards Siren. "Siren, you and Trinity see anything that catches your eye?"

"Nah, Boss, I'm good," Trinity says, snatching the almost empty bottle of Jack from Siren. "What's your plans? What are you going to do?" she asks, handing me the last drop of liquor.

I chug the last of the liquor courage and let out a groan before filling my girls' in on my plans.

Chapter 12: Ace

Now

Club music fills the air and I can only imagine the scene outside these walls. Brothers and the crowette's fucking and getting blowjobs all around. I'm in my office sipping on a glass of aged scotch, boots on my desk, and my mind off in another world of memories in the past. When a large noise comes from the main area of the clubhouse and the music suddenly stops. My office door is kicked open and a brown-haired woman manhandling one of my prospects comes in.

"On your knees, you little bitch," The woman yells, kicking Haas's feet out from under him, holding a knife to his neck. She glares at me and I'm sent back to when I was fourteen years old, knowing exactly who just busted in. My heart speeds up and my dick starts to harden in my jeans as I peer over at the now very adult, very sexy Kelsey, and how her breast fills out her very tight tank top.

"What the fuck are you doing, Kelsey?" I ask, as I jump out of my chair. "You can't treat my prospect like that and you just can't fucking show up like this."

"The fuck I can't!" She spits back, hatred filling her eyes. "Your prospect thinks it's ok to touch my ass without my permission. I have every right to treat him like this." She hauls back her leg and kicks him in the stomach.

"Where's Joker and BJ?" I ask Haas, who is kneeling, his eyes tearing up, and I swear he is about to piss himself.

"Oh, they are taking a little nap," Kelsey replies, kicking Haas to the floor. "Stay there you little shit or I'll cut off your dick and feed it to you!" Kelsey growls at the prospect as she strides over to my desk. She jumps on it, crossing her legs then picks up the name plaque that has my name and title on it. As if it's of no concern to her, she sits it back down.

"GOT A PROPOSITION FOR you, Ace," she says, with venom in her voice. "But first, what should I call you? Talon or Mr. President?" An evil grin takes over her face and it's a juxtaposition of beauty and fucking horror.

"You okay, boss? There's umm three ladies that joined the party with her," Zeus, like his namesake, is a big black God himself, says, as he stands six foot seven inches tall, muscles galore at my office door with an equally large muscular woman standing behind him, holding a gun to his back.

Zeus is a born killer and takes his duties as enforcer seriously and specializes in every weapon known to man. He's a loyal brother and one of the best men you could ever meet.

"Geez, Kels, call your girl's off. My guy's won't bother them," I say, striding up to Kelsey.

She laughs and glares at me like I'm a dumb fucker. "Tell your brothers we are cool and I'll tell my girls to back off. Then you and I will have a discussion." She jumps down from my desk, before turning around and smiling at me. "Ya know, like two old friends that need to catch up."

"Zeus, we're fine. Grab Haas, take his cut, and send him home," I order, as Zeus picks up Haas and throws the little prospect over his shoulder .

"He's like a black Hercules." The black haired woman says as she very obviously ogles Zeus, licking her lips, following him out of my office.

"Wrong Deity," I say, to the dark haired girl.

"Huh?" She turns around to face me.

"Not Hercules. His name is Zeus," I correct, as I cross my arms over my chest. "Hercules is the old man that sits at the bar with balding hair and one tooth."

"I can definitely see him making me say, Oh God!" The girl chortles exiting the room.

Chapter 13: Storm

Now

Talon was always cute when he was younger, but damn the man who stands before me today is nothing less than a sex God. His long black hair, strong chiseled jaw, nice nose and perfect cupid's bow lips are hot as can be but damn those blue eyes are fucking unbelievable. They are like a blue sky on a cloudless day; like they could suck the soul out of someone, or make an old friend's panties wet.

"So, I've heard about your mother. I'm sorry," Talon offers his condolences while grabbing my bicep and dragging me back to reality.

"I'm not." I deadpan and shrug my shoulders. "I haven't talked to her in over ten years, matter of fact that's sort of the reason I'm here," I admit, as I sit back down on Talon's desk.

"Storm," he whispers, as he runs a finger over the president patch on my leather cut. His voice is like rich, dark chocolate, tart but also sweet. It's deepend over the years, affecting me more than I care to admit."Let me guess how you got your road name, you come in like a storm and leave nothing but destruction in your path." His lip lifts at the corner with a smirk on his stupidly sexy face.

"That is me!" I reply, crossing my arms underneath my breast, noticing Talon eyeing my chest as my breast spills over the top of my tank-top. "They are nice aren't they? I've grown into them over the years," I say, peeking at my tits and making them bounce a little with my arms.

Talon looks me in the eyes. The pupils eclipse his irises with pure lust and groans a sexy animalistic growl that goes straight to my core.

"I've never been much of a tits man myself, but those I'm pretty sure can change my mind." His voice drips with unadulterated sex as he licks his lips. Once he comes to his senses, his gaze moves from my chest and he clears his throat.

"Oh, Mr. President, you can't handle all of this." I slap my thighs and realize that Talon is flirting with me. I'm a brazen hussy, because I'm flirting right back and I've only been around him for about thirty minutes.

I look away from him, pretending to check out his office. "Where is your crone, Mr. President? Where's your ol' lady? I'm sure she wouldn't like you hitting on me." A sarcastic smile crosses my face as I bat my eyelashes at him.

Once a member wants everyone to know they are in a committed relationship, they give them a property patch showing they belong to whoever they are with and that they find them as loyal partners.

He looks like he is about to choke on his scotch as he swigs what's left in the glass. "No Crone. No first lady. No ol' lady. No girlfriend. I'm single, Kelsey." His eyes turn to fire. "Is that how you want to reconnect?" he asks, as he stands in front of me. His hands grip the edge of his desk on either side of me effectively caging me in. The heat from his body rolls off him in waves. It's intoxicating being this close to him after all these years.

I stare up at him. "What do you mean, I want to reconnect?" Faux confusion drips from my words, because I know exactly what he's getting at, but I'm not ready to admit it to myself just yet.

"Sex," he says in a low tone, as his fingers rub circles on my thighs. His proximity makes me dizzy, the chemistry we used to have and the smell of his cologne. I hate how easy it is for him to turn me on, even after all these years.

"Are you fucking kidding me?" I snort, knocking his hand away and jumping off his desk. I can't let being near him confuse me or stop me from my mission. It's been ten years and time to make those from my past pay for what they did to me. "I haven't talked to you in a fucking decade and you're already thinking you can fuck me? You're as disgusting as your perverted father!" I call out over my shoulder, as I flounce to the door.

Before opening it though, I think better of leaving without sending him a message. I grab my hunting knife out of its sheath and stab it through the top of his desk all while looking Talon dead in his eyes. "The Murder of Crows owes me at least five blood debts and I will not leave until I collect." The weight of my words hit me and I know that nothing in this world, except for death will have me leaving this town, except for those who hurt me to pay.

Chapter 14: Ace

Now

"Why the fuck do my brother's owe you five blood debts, Kelsey? And never and I mean fucking never compare me to my old man, I'm nothing like him," I say, gazing at her like she's lost her damn mind. "No one has seen you since you were sixteen years old. There's no way that five of my brothers have killed five of your sisters, so explain." All the sexual tension from before has been completely sucked out of the room.

Kelsey straightens her back, juts her chin out, and an expression of pure evil comes over her beautiful face. "At least five of your brothers murdered Kelsey Weatherspoon the night of her seventeenth birthday. My sisters and I are here to collect the debt that's owed to her." Her eyes glisten with tears that I know she won't shed.

"Kelsey, you are right here. You aren't making any sense." I walk across the room to her and place my finger under her chin, tilting her face to look me in the eyes. "If we owe you the debt, we will gladly pay, but you're going to have to tell me what happened."

Kelsey sits on a love seat and kicks her boots up on a coffee table using her knife to clean invisible dirt from underneath her fingernails, her face is stone, and her eyes glass over as if she's mentally far away.

After an eternity, she opens her mouth. "I just wanted you, you know? I put on my new, sexy blue dress, did my hair and make up just right. I wanted to look beautiful just for you. I wanted to look amazing for when you showed your brothers you loved me and you were going to claim me in front of everyone. It's all I've wanted since I was twelve years old."

My heart thumps erratically in my chest and my hands are instantly sweaty. I have to rub them on my pants to remove the perspiration. Kelsey's face shows a frown as tears start to pool at her eyes, but she blinks them away. Her outer shell is harder than it was back then.

"I showed up at the party and one of your brothers, Jaxx and your dad said you were going to be back at any time and that I should just wait for you." She inhales a long deep breath. I can tell that she's lost in the memories of that night.

"Jaxx wouldn't accept no for an answer when I told him I didn't want to drink and the bartender that night made me a Jack and Coke. He was a prospect at the time. His name was Monster. Do you remember Monster? Is he still around?" she asks, but doesn't give me time to answer as she continues.

"I never thought they would hurt me, I sipped on the drink and waited for you. You never came though. When I got up to leave I was dizzy and couldn't move. Jaxx picked me up and took me to the room with the pool tables." Tears flowing freely from her eyes as she gazes across the room towards the door of the old billiards room.

"They took turns raping me Talon. Your dad, Jaxx, Monster, Dusty and more, some I didn't even know. They stole my life from me, they drugged me, beat me and raped me. I couldn't move. I couldn't scream. I had to lay there and do nothing, but pray you would come and stop them from hurting me." Kelsey sobs uncontrollably, hiding her face in her hands. That armor of hers finally cracking as the memory consumes her.

I pick her up into my arms, holding her close and kiss her forehead, telling her over and over that I am sorry. Even though I know my apology doesn't mean a fucking thing.

"I told my mother what had happened. She was under the influence of drugs and alcohol and you know what she did?" She pauses, looking up at me with tear filled eyes. It's almost as if we are teenagers again and we never grew up and the world around us never turned ugly. " She laughed." Her voice cracks and she laughs maniacally as she angrily swipes at her cheeks.

"She actually laughed and get this, she told me it was the club welcoming me in. She did nothing, but blamed me, and said it was my fault, so I left. I went to the hospital and they done a rape exam. I didn't tell them I knew some of the people who raped me at the hospital. I knew if the club could rape and beat me they could easily put a bullet in my head. I was in so much pain and had to make sure that nothing was going to kill me, that I wasn't internally bleeding and get a morning after pill. The exam confirmed that five men had raped me maybe more but since most wore condoms the five who didn't was the only DNA found. I was a virgin, Talon. I was saving myself for *you*, but that was stolen too."

She put her head on my chest, embarrassed to look at me now that the whole truth of that night is finally out. My chest grows tight, my hands involuntarily make a fist and I'm angrier than I've ever been in my life. I loved Kelsey with everything in me and when she left I lost a part of my soul. How could my father have done this? How could my brothers look me in the face after what they did to the person I loved?"

"I'll take it to church Kelsey, but no matter the vote, I'll help you get your justice. Your vengeance is my vengeance," I inform her as I wipe her tears away and kiss my girl's forehead.

Chapter 15: Kelsey

18...Then

"**H**ey Sam, I need a number 14!" God, I hate this job, slinging fried food to people all night long. My feet are killing me and I'm ready to go home. My last customer of the night looks homeless and smells of rotten garbage. I have to hold my breath as I serve his food.

"Sir, we are closing in ten minutes," I say, as I start getting the napkin holders refilled. *Just hurry the fuck up, mister.* I think to myself. I walk to the back to grab my purse and when I come back to the front the dirty man is gone.

"All clear, Sam. Goodnight." I slip out the door and down the alleyway to my studio apartment. The night is cool, and it's dark. There's a light thumping as if someone is walking behind me, but try to ignore them. *It's just my imagination.* I keep telling myself over and over.

Involuntarily, I speed up. My steps quickening as I come to the end of the alley. This isn't my usual route home. How did I get so turned around? In my near panic, a hand reaches out from the darkness and grabs me. I try to scream, but I can't. Whoever pulled me into the shadows covers my mouth.

The blood is pumping so fast in my veins I can hear it rushing in my ears. I'm anxious, but I know that I'm going to have to defend myself and run. The guy turns me facing him, hands holding mine to my side. I headbutt him as hard as I can. There's a crunch and a warm shower spray on my face. I've busted his nose. I kick him in the groin, causing him to groan and double over. Taking the opportunity, I run as fast as I can away from the guy.

The feet pound against the pavement and my side burns from exertion, but I am too slow. I'm pulled down to the ground. He grabs me again, and I fight, scratch, and kick him, but he only tightens his grasp. A whimper escapes my throat as I struggle. My muscles are burning from the losing battle against this stranger. Something stabs my leg in the struggle though, and I remember my switchblade. I pull it out of my pocket and slice his forearm. He stumbles back. His eyes are wide in shock as he looks down at the nasty cut I gave him. This is my chance. I just to my feet and jab the knife into his neck. Blood squirts from his jugular, splashing my neck and chest. It's warm like standing under a hot shower.

I'm paralyzed as I look down at the man who thought he could snatch me up. It's the guy from the restaurant. Crimson that looks black in the night, spurts from his mouth as he chokes on his own blood. When the light in his eyes dies and his mouth is stuck in a frozen cry for help, I scream for help, but of course no one comes. I'm all alone.

My thighs and lungs burn as I run the rest of the way to my apartment. There is blood all over me that's now dry and itchy. As soon as I jolt through the door, I sling my stained shirt into the trash and race to the shower to scrub the remaining gore off of me.

My fingerprints are all over the knife. I have to go back. I have to get that knife or they'll put me in jail. I pull at the roots of my hair. *Fuck. Fuck. Fuckity. Fuck.* I dry myself off and grab some fresh clothes to throw on.

The night is still young as I rush back to the alley where I'd stabbed my attacker, but he's gone, disappeared. There is no blood, and no body. Did my anxiety riddled mind make it up? At least, I didn't murder him. I'm not a killer, *yet*.

Chapter 16: Storm

B anging on the door wakes me up from a dreamless sleep. "Boss, are you okay in there?" The deep voice of Chyna on the other side jerks me to life as I remember the night before. I must've cried myself to sleep, sitting on Talon's lap. While he held me. *Oh shit!*

"Yeah, Chyna girl, I'm up," I yell, lifting my head off the couch.

"Just making sure you are okay!" She bellows. Her steps grow more distant the further she walks off down the hallway.

I scan around the room. Talon's room. Wait, I'm not in his office anymore. He must've carried me to his bed after I fell asleep.

The bedroom is plain with no details of any personality at all. Just basic necessities. The bathroom just has men's toiletries, and no decorations on the walls or anything showing Talon's individuality. I open his closet to find jeans, tee shirts, and a few pairs of boots. That's all that is in there. *Maybe he has another place where he lives, there's no way he stays here all the time.*

One of my girls must've brought my bags in for me. I take an old crumpled up picture of Talon and me and stick it up on his dresser mirror. It's of happier times. I'm wondering what Talon will do when he sees it though. The fact that I've kept it this whole time has to mean something.

After the long ride here, my skin feels as if there's a layer of dust covering it. I should take a well deserved hot shower to wash off the road dirt and the shame of having to relive my past.

I put on a pair of black tight jeans and a lacey red bra and black tank top. My hair is long now so I run a comb through it and tie it in a messy bun on top of my head. I apply some cherry chapstick. This is my go to look these days, nothing sexy or hot. Just me. I check my phone and send a text to Bear and Quinn to check on things before heading downstairs to find Talon.

As I make my way through the main room of the clubhouse to the kitchen, I pause at the room to the right, the billiard room. My stomach flip flops as a wave of nausea hits me. Nope, never ever stepping foot in there. I shiver, holding my arms over my chest and mosey on to the dining area where Siren and Trinity are eating with Talon and a few other guys.

"What are you guys doing?" I ask, eyeing Siren as she takes a bite of toast.

"I ask them to eat breakfast." Talon pops up from his chair and remarks, "I let you sleep in and the big girl..."

"Chyna," I correct.

"Chyna, right. Wouldn't leave your door. She guarded you like you're a treasure." His eyes run up and down my body and he clears his throat. "Which of course, you are," he admits, shooting me a sexy grin.

"Chyna is a dedicated vice president," I say, with a smile. "She's also a famous body builder."

He nods his head in appreciation and gestures to a seat. "We have some information for you, Kels. I mean *Storm*, to help with your mission. First get you some breakfast. You and your girls' can meet me and my counsel in the war room in an hour." He grabs his plate and takes it to the kitchen.

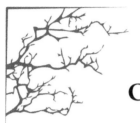

Chapter 17: Ace

"Oh shit!" I hear as I stroll out of the bathroom wearing nothing but a towel. Kelsey's face is blood red, her jaw drops. She's clearly ogling me, but she quickly turns around, hiding her face.

"Sorry, I needed something out of my bag," she says after clearing her throat and starts digging in her bag again.

I rub my hand down my chest as I walk into my closet and grab a shirt and a pair of jeans. "It's okay, baby doll. I ain't got nothing you've never seen before. I mean it's bigger and I'm more toned." The towel I'm wearing falls to the floor as Kelsey turns around to say something, but nothing comes out of her mouth. Her jaw hangs open as I walk up to her. My naked cock almost rubs into her pussy. "What's the matter? You like what you see? " I grip the back of her neck and she closes her pouty mouth, staring up at me through her lashes. "I've been thinking about your lips all morning. "

Kelsey inhales a small breath as I pull her in. My cock now digging into her, and semi-hard. I lick her lips wanting full access to her mouth. She turns to putty in my arms, welcoming my tongue as it massages hers. A groan of pleasure escapes her but I capture it with my lips. Grabbing hold of the backs of her knees, I wrap her legs around my waist and deepen our kiss. My now full hardon rubs against her jeans. Her body trembles as my hand moves slowly against her sensitive skin under her shirt. Her nipples are hardened peaks through her lacy bra. The desperate urge to see them on full display has me slipping her shirt over head, in one quick swoop. With one hand, I unclasp her bra, letting her bountiful breast fall free.

Storm's body suddenly goes rigid in my arms and she pushes against my chest, causing me to release her.. As soon as her feet hit the floor, she snatches her shirt, throws it on and runs out of my room. The sudden turn of events leaves me speechless. I didn't even have time to collect my bearings and stop her or ask her what was wrong. *I fucked up.* I run my fingers through my damp hair. *Fuck.*

Chapter 18: Storm

I rush out of the room and down the stairs. My breathing is erratic and I can't slow them down in this state of panic. Talon's taste still remains on my lips like the taste of liquor after a hearty swig. It's tempting and dangerous all at the same time. My destination is unwavering as I run out the front door and towards my bike.

Breathe, damn it. What the fuck is wrong with me? It's Talon. He is not going to hurt me. Why did all of a sudden my body have a fight or flight response to what we were doing? I want him, don't I? I've always wanted Talon, and I've always wanted him to want me. So what the fuck is my problem when this is exactly what I've always dreamed of since we were kids shooting bottles in the backyard?

My name is a tornado siren on the wind and I peer back at the clubhouse, where the sound is located. It's Talon and Chyna yelling for me to come back. My senses are overwhelmed. I need to get out. I wave my hand and jump on my bike. I just need a ride, a few minutes to clear my head and get back on the mission.

The whole reason for me being here is about the blood debts that are owed to me, not a fuck session with the son of one of my rapists. The wind whips my loose strands in all directions and my phone vibrates in my pocket, of which I both ignore. I just concentrate on the feel of my bike between my legs, the feel of the air that rushes over my bare skin and soon it calms me.

Riding has always soothed me. I can take my mind off my problems and think about nothing but the road ahead with no destination. I do have one this time though. The old trailer that should've been taken out by a tornado, but not even I could be that lucky. I get off my bike, unlock the door and go inside. The tears come. Tears that should've been cried years ago but were never shed. The years of pain, hurt, and abandonment finally hit me. I grab the Louisville slugger that is by the door and swing it at anything and everything that is breakable. I haul the baseball bat and smash the television sending glass everywhere. After I wear myself down, I sink down on the old couch and just let the tears flow. I curl up into a ball and cry myself asleep.

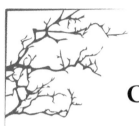

Chapter 19: Ace

FUCK. I completely messed up. Now She's gone and won't answer anyone's calls. I squeeze the cold pack in my fist, crushing the ice within to make it more comfortable against my tender eye. Damn that Chyna has a mean left hook. I can't believe she punched me after Kelsey went running out like a bat out of hell. It took everything within me to not turn into a beast and roar at the world around me. This isn't a situation I asked for. I wish I could go back in time and kill everyone of those motherfuckers that touched her and stop her from leaving me. We were screwed over from the start and maybe I pushed her to connect too fast after all these years. There's some part of me that deserves it though, because I didn't try hard enough to search for her that night. She was here right under my nose the whole time.

My free hand clenches at my side the more I think about what I could've, should've done differently as I wait for the room to fill up so we can start the meeting. Chyna went to look for Storm, at least, so that relieves some of the tension building up with worry in my shoulders. The only thing left for me to do is let the rest of the club know what's going on. Church must go on so we can figure out the plan of action.

The council crowds into the room, all in an uproar over all the excitement that has occurred as of last. I bang the gavel against the table to get the attention of my brothers. "Yo, Prez looks like ya got a love tap. Was the sex that kinky?" Zeus asks, before cracking up laughing.

"No, fuck nugget, Chyna decided that my face was too good looking and punched me in the eye," I say, giving him a shut-the-fuck up scowl.

"Listen, I need a few volunteers to go on a ride with me and Storm's club to help her with her debt." My fucking father played apart in this. I clench the edges of the table in an attempt to restrain the anger that's boiling in my blood. "Some of y'all will stay here and run the club while we are away." I glance around the room at my brothers. This is a personal matter, and I'm wanting to see who will volunteer to right this wrong before I start calling names.

"Prez. Tell me what you need and I'll do it," Murphy says, while glaring among the council. He must feel the same as I do since he's VP.

"Me too." The others say one after another and I can feel the pride in my chest rising. I know I picked the right people for my council members. These are my brothers. My ride or dies through and through.

After about an hour of discussing our plans and determining the location of the old members, we decide that Murphy and Cash are going to stay and take care of the club house. The rest of the council is going with me and Storm's girls. It's time to be better than my father, time to be a good man, but I know that I'd be killing my brothers and that stings my heart just a little.

I end the meeting, grab my phone, and shoot a text off to Storm.

ME: All set. We know where Monster is. We'll leave tomorrow.

Chapter 20: Storm

"**B**oss, you here?" The voice arouses me from sleep. There's a sharp pain in my neck when I move. It must be in knots from the way I fell asleep on this old sofa.

"Yeah, Chyna, come on in," I say, trying to adjust my eyes to the dark. I switch on the only lamp I didn't destroy and see Chyna's muscular form standing in the doorway. "Get in here, Chyna, I'm okay."

"I popped Talon in the eye. It's black," she confesses, taking a seat in the chair next to the couch.

"Why?" I glare, feeling a little defensive over Talon. "He didn't do anything, I freaked out and ran out on him." A smile spreads across my face at the thought of Chyna punching Talon for me. It's kind of funny actually.

"I didn't know. You ran out of there like a bat out of hell. I assumed he did something." She shrugs her shoulders, not at all bothered by her actions.

"Eh, don't worry about it, I'm sure he deserves it for one reason or another."

I glance down at my phone that's sitting on the coffee table. The screen lights up showing ten new calls and twenty-five new messages.

The first thing I do is read through the text from Talon. Butterflies flutter, batting their wings in my stomach. That's excitement, I feel. This is really happening. I look at Chyna with the biggest grin that nearly cracks my face in two. "It's on Sister. Tomorrow we are going after Monster. Let the rest of the girls know." I stand up from the couch, stretching out the tightness in my muscles.. "For now though, let's head back to the club house. I need to talk to Talon." I gather up my belongings and say a quiet goodbye to the piece of shit house I grew up in and to my mother. May she rot and get feasted on by worms in her eternal slumber. I step out onto the porch, lock the door, and head to my bike, never giving the shack another glance.

That house and the memories locked inside are my past. I'm working on taking back what was taken from me. Starting tomorrow, I will soon have my vengeance and will never have to look back again.

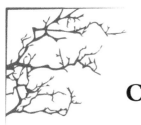

Chapter 21: Ace

I shower, brush my teeth, run a comb over my hair, and throw on gray jogging pants to sleep in. My stomach is in knots, worrying over Kelsey. I hope I hear from her soon. I text the others to be ready at five a.m. Kissimmee Saint Cloud, Florida was a while away and that's where that bastard Monster has been living.

After turning down the bed, I climb in beneath the comforter. I haven't changed the bed sheets and the smell of Kelsey's shampoo lingers on the pillow. The aroma of strawberries and mint flood my nostrils and a vivid vision of the heated kiss we shared immediately comes to mind. The way her lips taste, the plumpness of them, the curve of her body pressing into mine. The memory causes my dick to harden. I shove my hand into my pants and grip my shaft firmly, pumping myself and picturing Kelsey's immaculate, juicy lips wrapped around my cock. Her warm mouth taking my large dick and it hitting the back of her throat. Her eyes gazing up at me as I watch her consuming me. A low moan escapes me just before I hear a knock at my door.

"Fuck, Zeus!" I growl, pissed off that I was interrupted.

"It's not Zeus. It's Storm." A small whispered voice chimes through my bedroom door.

I jerk my hand out of my pants. "Just a minute." I sit straight up, praying my hardon away. I climb out of bed and rearrange myself, tucking my shaft in the waistband of my sweats. I'm still standing at half mast, but it'll have to be okay. Maybe she won't notice. I fling open the door to see a sad-faced Kelsey.

"Glad to see you came back." I step back and give her just enough space to squeeze into my room. "Come on in." Her body rubs against mine and I have to stifle to groan that's threatening to escape my throat. This woman is going to be the death of me.

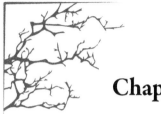

Chapter 22: Storm

I step into his bedroom, my front gliding against his. Ace is so attractive. He was a handsome boy back in the day, but the guy standing before me is all man. I can't help but stare at his ripped tattooed chest, tight strong shoulders, and his thick jaw line. My eyes continue inspecting him all over and my face heats when I notice his dick is hard.

"Sorry, I just came here to tell you I'm back, and that I'm sorry for running out on you." I glance at the wall, anywhere to keep from looking at him.

"It's okay Kelsey, you don't owe me an explanation. Look it's late, why don't you climb into my bed. I'll take the floor. We have an early start tomorrow and I think we both need some rest." He grabs a pillow from the bed.

"We are both adults. You can sleep in the bed with me," I urge as I remove my jacket and my boots.

"Okay." He straightens the covers back up and sits down on the bed.

I get in from the other side, and lay down on my side with my back to him.

"Goodnight," I say, pulling the covers around me.

He pulls me to his chest and places an arm around me. "Goodnight, Babe."

He breathes in my ear and I feel his chest rise and fall against my back. His cock rubs against my ass. I move to distance myself from him, but he doesn't allow that to happen. His grip tightens on my waist, pulling me to him.

"Just calm the fuck down and go to sleep. I'm not going to try anything, I just want to be close." I start to relax next to him. The man who I loved all through my childhood, the teenager I was in love with, and my best friend. It takes hearing his even breaths and the rise and fall of his chest before I finally fall asleep with his arms enveloping me. The only man whose arms I've ever slept in.

Chapter 23: Ace

My phone is going off, the alarms buzzing non-stop. I feel for Kelsey in the bed, but she isn't there. I sit up instantly. My shoulders bunching with panic until I hear the shower running. I situate my morning wood and check my phone. There's texts from Price letting me know that we are set to go. That's my cue to get moving. I stand up and stretch, thinking about going to the bathroom and joining her, but deciding that a blade in my gut probably isn't worth seeing her naked. I seriously have to piss though, so I hope she hurries up.

I pick out a clean black shirt, a pair of black jeans and put them on. I slip on my cut and hear the door opening behind me.

"Price says the bikes are ready to go, says your girl Trinity has yours ready too," I inform, as I let my eyes sweep over her sexy curves.

Price loves anything to do with motorcycles and the road. He is the road captain, he makes sure on all runs we have a clear way without the trouble of other clubs, which roads to take and any stops needed made along the way. He also makes sure all bikes are up to snuff and helps run our legit businesses. He is a tall motherfucker and well muscled with tattoos covering his body. His twin brother is Cash and the only way you can tell them apart besides the different tattoos is the scar from Price's right eye down his chin and Cash's different colored eyes.

"I know, I talked to her already. Gonna put on my shoes and grab a cup of coffee then we'll be ready to ride. I watch as she puts her cut on and the look of pride as she rakes her fingers over the patch. She's so fucking beautiful, always has been, even as an annoying kid, she was cute.

"See you down stairs," she calls, heading to the door, grabbing a bag on her way out.

A cup of coffee is made for me when I go downstairs. I write the guys and tell them to be ready to leave in ten.

"You ready Kel..., Storm?" I ask, grabbing my bag.

"Been ready for years," she answers, as she puts on some sunglasses and heads out the clubhouse doors.

Chapter 24: Storm

Both road captains give a clear run all the way through. We know where it is appropriate to run our colors and where not to. We decide to break halfway in Toomsboro, Georgia, where we can refuel and eat, and rest for a few.

There's a small seafood diner in the area called Thompson's Cove where we decide to stop. The look on the staff and customers' faces as we pile in are hilarious. I'm pretty sure they have never seen a group of bikers before.

We all order our food and settle into eating fried catfish dinners, shrimp, and hushpuppies. I've always been a hushpuppy lover.

"Trinity, are we doing good with time?" I ask, stuffing shrimp into my mouth like it was my last meal.

"All good Prez, I gave us an hour and a half here then a clear shot to Florida. We have rooms waiting on us at the Budget Inn for the night, once we get there."

"Good job, thank you." I have to give Trinity more acknowledgement than I do, she really is efficient at getting her shit done.

I look over at Ace, but he is in a deep conversation with Zeus. I take one last swallow of my soda, and head to the restroom. I urinate and wash my hands, deciding to throw water on my face, removing any road dirt off and stroll outside.

Our bikes completely take over the small parking area. I chuckle to myself as I stroll over to my bike. I dig into my pannier for some chapstick, run a brush through my hair and just soak in the sun, entranced in my own world. I'm so lost in thought that I don't even hear the footsteps approaching behind me until Ace's voice booms, knocking me out of my euphoric state.

"YOU ALRIGHT?!"

"Yeah, I'm good. Just throwing some chapstick on and enjoying the nice weather." He steps closer to me, his eyes skim over my body and a smile comes across his face. When I notice his ogling, I punch him in the stomach. "Stop looking at me like you could eat me, Ace."

"Oh, but what a treat you would be." He grants me with a wolfish grin that would even give little red a run for her money before he strides away toward his bike, as the others pile out of the diner. I picture what his mouth would feel like on my most intimate parts, but quickly shake those thoughts out of my head. I've more important things to worry about.

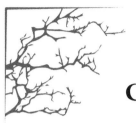

Chapter 25: Ace

The motel we stop at to rest for the night is just across the Florida border. We all go to our own rooms, except I notice that Chyna and Zeus are sneaking into the room across from mine. Well, that's definitely none of my business.

I swipe the card and wait for the greenlight before opening the door. My room is small, and I'd assume all of the rooms are the same. A bed, an ugly painting of a field over it, a chest of drawers, one table, and one chair, and a small bathroom fill the space. I toss my bag on the bed and kick off my boots. All I want is a good, hot shower to wash off the day's road dirt and get some sleep. I start to undress, but there's a knock on my door.

"Talon, are you asleep?" It's Kelsey's lyrical voice on the other side. I open the door to her arms crossed over her chest, accentuating her assets that I can't seem to stop admiring.. "Can I come in?"

I swing the door open a little more, just so she has enough room to get by me, but she has to touch me to come in.

"Whatcha need, Kels?" I ask, turning to face her and closing the door behind me. "A kiss goodnight?"

Her face turns red as her eyes roam over my chest and stop at the V at my hips. She licks her kissable, sexy lips and shakes her head as if she was making herself come out of a trance.

"No, I want to make sure we are set up for tomorrow, " she says, as she sits on my bed.

"Yes, Dollface, everything is ready. Your girls are in charge and my guys are back up. You'll have your vengeance on Monster."

Her eyes shine with unshed tears. I saunter over to her and kneel at her feet. "Look at me, Kels." With my finger like I did before, I raise her chin up so I can peer into her eyes. But Storm doesn't hold my gaze for long before she moves her head from my hand and pulls me closer to her. She lays on my chest. "You just take what you need from me. Okay?" She nods, nuzzling her cheeks against my pecs. I hold her quietly to me, letting her end the embrace when she's ready to do so. About five minutes later, Storm releases me and stands up. I push a stray hair behind her ear, because I don't want to stop touching her, but I know she won't stay. She places a kiss on my cheek and exits out of my hotel room.

The shower is calling my name, the smell of Kelsey is all over me and I can't help but to stroke my shaft. The original course I had before she barged into my room the other day. With the water running over the back of my head, I pump my cock in my fist. The idea of her beneath me sends a building pressure in my lower spine. Her breast bouncing with each hard thrust, moving her up in the bed beneath me. "Fuck, that's it baby," I groan still imagining it's her pussy wrapped around around my veiny shaft instead of my hand. My hips thrust into my palm and my release comes fast as I come all over the shower drain.

I may not have her yet, but I do know one thing Storm's my girl and I'll make her my ol' lady. I have patience, I've waited this long, I can wait as long as it takes to make her mine again.

Chapter 26: Storm

The smell of Talon's cologne is thick on me, I love his mix of peppermint and smoke. It calms me. I remove my clothes and head into the shower, letting the hot water relax my muscles. I get so tense on long rides. The water feels so amazing. It's hot enough to turn my skin a fiery red. Even though the shower is burning away every scent from my flesh, all I can do is picture Talon.

The way he holds me so tight and kisses me like I'm the only woman in the world, or the way his body felt pressed against mine. I run my fingers over my breast, squeezing my hardening nipples before moving my hand down my stomach to my pussy. My abs jump with the light touch and my core clenches in anticipation. I run my digits through my lips, teasing myself a little before massaging my clit. The tension in my core builds and a moan escapes my lips. I'm in need of a release. The electricity throbs in my bundle of nerves. I insert my fingers, thrusting them, coating my wetness on them. My vagina tightens, quivers as I imagine that thick corded length that was pressed against my center in his room. The whole time I'm finger fucking myself I'm wishing it was Talon's fingers inside of me. I orgasm picturing my hands using his chest for leverage as I ride his cock. The intensity of my orgasm hits me and my pussy clenches in a rhythmic pulse around my fingers. My free hand slaps against the shower wall as I slump over, spent. I quickly wash my hair and body and climb out, wrapping a towel around me.

I need to get control of myself. I can't let my lust get in the way of my vengeance. I need this, like I need air to breathe. I quickly brush my teeth and hair and climb into bed. Tomorrow is going to be a long day. Tomorrow, I'll make Monster pay for drugging me, for taking my trust and throwing it back in my face. Tomorrow is the beginning of my vengeance and it'll send a message to the others. That I know for sure.

I WAKE UP TO MY PHONE alarm blasting, Divide the Day's "Fuck Away the Pain" and click it off. First, coffee. The little coffee pot is easy to work, just throw the water in and pop in the already made coffee filter. I stretch my body, and put on my clothes for the day. A pair of black lace boy shorts, matching Bra-let, a black tee and denim jeans, and of course, my black biker boots to complete the look. I brush out my long hair and put it in a ponytail at the nape of my neck.

I better text my girls so they can get up and get ready too. It's gonna be a long day, and blood will be shed tonight. I'm almost giddy at the thought of what all I'm going to do to Monster.

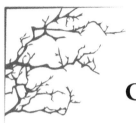

Chapter 27: Ace

"So, Siren is going to go into the bar where Monster is bartending. An old dive called The Anchor, and do what she does best, use her sexiness to lure him outside. Zeus will be waiting outside the door and will hit him with a quick dose of ketamine, to knock him out and we'll get him in our van to the abandoned barn in Northern Osceola County," Storm instructs, when we stop at a gas station and take a bathroom break.

Bones raises his hand as if he's in class, which is surprising because I have yet to hear him speak, since we've been on the road. "How do you know Monster will be interested in Siren?"

Bones is one creepy motherfucker. He's easily the smallest physically of all my brothers. He is almost six and a half feet tall and slender. He has obsessive compulsive Disease and a fetish for bleach. He is never not wearing gloves since he's also a germaphobe. Sanitizer is a must, hell he probably uses it as his cologne. He was a chemical engineer and has a degree in forensic science. Not only does he make sure no DNA can be found, but the fucker can dispose of bodies where they will never be traced.

"No worries about that Bonesy-wonesy," Siren coos as she walks out of the girls' restroom to join us. Her new outfit consists of the shortest barely there skirt with a bikini top as a shirt, looking as though she's getting ready to do a porno or a majorly hot biker spread. Her now high heels clicking the ground as she sways to her bike and removes a sucker, popping it between her lush full lips. The mere display of her performance already has Bones licking his lips as she sucks the lollipop and gazes at him with innocent bedroom come-fuck-me eyes.

"Right," Bones says, clearing his throat. "I see no problem with you getting him out of there." He ogles her over one more time and turns his head, as if he's disgusted at his own thoughts.

"Any questions? Anything to add?" I say, treading towards my bike, but no one says anything. "Okay, let's meet at the bar."

Chapter 28: Storm

"It's fucking humid," I say, out loud to anyone that will listen. I run my fingers through my hair and put it up in a messy bun. The truth is I'm hella excited. I cannot wait to dish out Monster's punishment for helping steal my innocence and ruining my life.

Siren has been inside for about thirty minutes. The Anchor should be calling last call at any time and the bar will be closing in another hour or so. Butterflies flutter in my stomach and anticipation hits me hard. I can barely stay still and not look excited. Ace's club and I are hidden in the back of the old run down bar so Monster can't see us and know who we are. Ace tries to talk to me, but I can't focus on anything but what is about to go down.

The thoughts of making Monster suffer in so many different ways is making me all tingly on the inside. I don't think I've ever been so happy to plan out a murder as I am right now.

Chyna and Zeus are getting along well, which surprises me to be honest. I always thought that Chyna was into chicks not dicks, but hey, whatever rocks her boat. Zeus is a good looking man, tall and bulky like a bodybuilder and skin the color of ebony. He always has a big beautiful smile that lights up his face, making him look young. Good for her. I'm happy she's getting laid.

The Anchor's main lights go out, showing the bar is now closed. Siren messages me that they're about to come out the back employee's doors and everyone is already in their places. The van is pulled up close to the back and Zeus is standing just beside the door where it'll be easy to grab Monster and stick him with the syringe full of horse tranquilizer.

Muffled voices come from inside the bar. Siren comes out first, following behind her is a huge Monster about six foot six with gigantic muscles and black, long, oily hair. He sure hasn't gotten better looking these last few years. Zeus pounces on him like a wild cat, getting him in his jugular vein with the syringe. Monster swings his arms and begins to kick at Zeus who is as big as he is, if not bigger. The ketamine kicks in within seconds which sends Monster face first into the pavement.

"We better get this show on the road. No telling how long the ketamine will last on his big ass." Bones and Zeus pick up the large body and throw him in the back of the van. Bones climbs in the back of the van with Monster. Zeus has the keys to the van which he will be driving and we follow him out of The Anchors parking lot and travel the twenty-three miles to the abandoned barn that is set up as a torture and killing room.

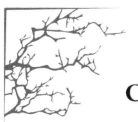

Chapter 29: Ace

The barn that we're using tonight is falling apart. An old piece of property that has been vacant for fifteen years. The roof is half gone and the wood is rotting. The smell of cows and horses is in the air from a farm that's about a mile down the road. The ground is muddy and the squishing noises are loud as we dredge from our bikes to the dilapidated barn.

Storm's mood is giddy as she watches Bones and Zeus carry Monster's big ass out of the van. He's out cold still, the stank of stale liquor, and body odor pouring off of him is nearly bad enough to turn your stomach. The rest of the council are keeping watch around the area to make sure no one is sniffing around or tries to pull up on what's about to go down. Storm's girls are out there too, besides Chyna, who's always usually only a few feet away from Storm and always on guard.

Zeus places Monster on a metal chair that's covered with plastic. The whole room has sheets of clear plastic around everything. He zip ties Monster's legs and arms. A big metal chain secures him to the seat that is connected to the barn. His frame barely sits straight. The Monster's head is dangling, looking as if he's already dead.

"How much of the tranquilizer did you give him?" I step closer to Monster examining him. I can barely remember him from my teens. He's way older, gray hair mixed with black and a face full of wrinkles. He has to be in his late fifties or sixties by now.

"You ready?" I ask Storm, as she coughs up a huge expectorate and spits it right in Monster's face. "I guess that's a yes." I nod to Bones to wake him up with the ammonium carbonate smelling salts.

Chapter 30: Storm

I'm as happy as a kid on Christmas day. Bones puts the smelling salts under Monster's nose, breaking it open, jolting him awake. He keeps trying to free himself from the ties but can't. He can't scream either, his mouth is stuffed with a rag found from a stall in the barn and duct taped closed. He looks around himself, taking in his surroundings. His eyes are wide and wild when he spots Ace and then me.

The look of confusion on his face pisses me off. My appearance hasn't changed over the years all that much, surely this fucker knows who I am. He knows Ace because his eyes keep following him.

"Hey, hey, hey. You piece of shit. Look at me! Not at him." I snap my fingers in his face. He swings his head in my direction, mumbling something I can't understand.

"Do you remember who I am?" I say, glaring at him in his dead, gray eyes. "Do you remember drugging me at a birthday party at the M.O.C club house about ten years ago? Where you and your buddies got off on beating and raping me?" I turn my back to him and pull out a hammer. I slap the cold metal face of the hammer against my hand.

"Do you see, Ace? You know your brother? The President? He granted me vengeance and it all starts with you!" I scream, as I whack him in the left knee, causing a mumbling noise of pain and discomfort on the prick's face. "If you would have never drugged my drink, none of it would have happened. I was a seventeen year old kid" I slam the other knee with the hammer, a gut-wrenching crunch radiates in the air, causing a satisfying feeling to wash over me.

"I'll give you one chance to give your side of the story. I'm gonna have Zeus remove the gag and if you make any noise that's above the

84

sound of my voice I'll rip your tongue out. Do you understand me?" The nasty fucker nods his head and Zeus removes the gag.

I exchange the hammer I used for breaking Monster's kneecaps for a hunting knife. I hold the blade against his neck. "I'm going to ask you questions, and you'll answer them or I'll jam this knife into your jugular. Do you understand me?"

"Y-yes," he stammers.

"Why did you mess with my drink?" I say, pushing the knife into the flesh of his throat.

"P-Prez. H-he tttold me too. sssaid you were a little bbbitch and needed to be tttaught a lesson," he stutters, sweat pouring from his face.

"It never happened to cross your mind that I was an underage child. I was seventeen fucking years old! You shouldn't be drugging anyone! Let alone a fucking kid!" I snarl.

I put the dirty rag back in his mouth and re-secure the tape across his mouth. It was pure fucking rage bringing the knife up and stabbing him over and over marking his body with cuts not caring where my blade goes in. Blood squirts and pours from his body and flies in my face, but I don't care. I stab and stab until I can't hold my arms up any longer and the knife falls at my feet. Blood sprays the plastic covered walls and all over Zeus, Bones and Chyna. We're all covered in rapist blood.

I trudge over to Ace and bring his lips to mine. I kiss him, our tongues swirling and tasting each other like it was the first time. I want him, I can feel it in the pit of my stomach, and he wants me too. There's no better feeling than that of becoming one step closer to freeing the burdens of the past.

Ace gathers me in his arms, before telling the others to clean up the mess and make sure that Bones disposes of the body. Apparently, he has a special formula that gets rid of bodies as well. I think I need to have him and Quinn compare notes. After the short hike to the bikes, Ace sets me down on his motorcycle and gets my helmet off my bike.

"You are riding back with me," he informs me, tightening the straps on my helmet. I like when he talks in his bossy tone, it sends a trill straight to my clit. I simply nod my head moving to the back of the motorcycle seat, so he can get on. I wrap my arms around him when he starts up his bike and a feeling of deja vu hits me, from days of our past.

One down, four more to go.

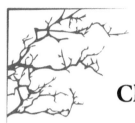

Chapter 31: Storm

As soon as the hotel room door closes, I attack Ace. He stands no chance of fighting me off. I climb up his body like a tree. I wrap my legs around his thick muscled body and kiss him like it would save my life. I've never felt this need before, this want of pure adrenaline and sex.

Covered in the blood of one of my rapists, knowing I took his life is an empowering feeling. I've taken many lives over the years, but nothing has ever made me feel like this.

Ace carries me to the bed and slowly undresses me. He glides my shirt over my head then my bra letting them hit the ground. When he goes for my pants and panties, I ease my hips off the bed so he can tug them both off. He gets on his knees like I'm an altar and he's praying for forgiveness. He begins by kissing and licking my legs on both sides, until he gets to my inner thighs where there's a sharp sting of pain. I look down as he sinks his teeth into my sensitive flesh, biting and sucking me in. Leaving his mark on me, claiming me as his. He gently kisses the marks he leaves behind. I watch as he pulls my hips closer to him, gripping me possessively. His tongue starts at my ass and licks me all around my sensitive mound.

"Eat me, Ace," I beg, as I grab his hair and push his face into my pussy. He responds with a guttural growl into my sex and wraps his sexy lips around my throbbing clit and sucks it so hard, I'm engulfed in euphoric pleasure.

He puts two fingers inside of me, curling them, massaging my g-spot. The feeling is too much with his mouth on my clit and his fingers moving inside me. "I'm going to come," I mewl, like a cat in heat, as he bites my clit and sends me over the edge. The world goes dark and I see stars as I chase my release.

He removes his fingers from me. My come shining and stretching among his fingers. He shows me the fruit of his labor, his eyes never leaving mine as he licks them clean. "That was the hottest thing I had ever seen in my life," I remark ,watching as he smirks and climbs over me and kisses me passionately with the taste of me still on his lips.

"I HAVE WANTED TO TASTE you for so fucking long, Dollbaby. You taste like raspberries and cream. God, Babe, I need to be in you now." He spreads my legs, opening me up wide. His gaze heats my sex. "You look better than I could've ever imagined."

He maneuvers his body between them. He gathers more of my wetness from my pussy and rubs it on his girthy, throbbing cock. His forearms cage me in and he whispers huskily in my ear, "But you'll look even better when I claim you and you're dripping with my come."

His words send a shiver down my spine and my cunt clenches in anticipation of being filled to the brim and stretched. There's a heart beat of time. Moment when all the bad shit vanishes and all the years we spent apart never existed. Then he slams into me in one quick succession causing me to groan with pleasure.

He keeps whispering how beautiful I am. How I feel so good milking his cock dry with my tight pussy. How much he wants me and I was all he's ever wanted, but I'm lost in my own pleasure and feelings to grasp the meaning of his words, as he fucks me. My legs are wrapped around his waist, holding on as he thrusts into me. Our chests rub against each other with the movement and I arch my back more to feel the friction against my hardened nipples.

"More, Talon, more" I cry, meeting his hips flesh to desperate flesh. Both of us climbing the mountain, ready to leap from the edge. "I'm so close, baby."

I clutch his forearms, holding on to him as he reaches down between us and pinches my clit. It's like a zap of electrocution to my core.

"Oh, god," I moan before biting down on his shoulder as I come all over his dick, leaving my own mark on him.

"That's right, baby, I'll be your savior when you need me," he growls, "but I'd rather be the devil on your shoulder as you burn this world to the *fucking* ground for what they did to you." His own rhythm becomes erratic, harder and deeper with every slap of skin. Until his body grows rigid, stilling above, and a deep groan reverberates through his chest as he reaches his orgasm.

"Fuck, Kels," he whispers with my name on his lips as he falls over me and to the side pulling me with him. "That was worth the wait."

After a few minutes, he gets up and goes to the bathroom, running water can be heard. When he comes back in the room, he lifts me up and carries me to the big, jacuzzi tub and sets me in it. He climbs in behind me, causing water to slosh over the side of the tub, soaking the floor. He wets my hair and puts in shampoo, and I relax into him, letting him clean me up. Letting him take care of me.

"Is this the first time since?" he says, as he rinses the soap from my hair. I know what he means. Was it my first time having sex since the rape? It had been. I've had no desire to be with anyone sexually since it happened and just nod my head, yes. He doesn't say anything else as he washes both our bodies and dries us off before carrying me back to his bed. He pulls me close to him, wrapping his arms around my body. I settle into his embrace and before I know it, I'm asleep.

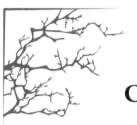

Chapter 32: Ace

The next morning, to my suprise, my bed is empty. Storm left without as much as a goodbye. Well, this is going to be an odd ride to the next place of revenge. Dusty. Dusty is next on the list. He lives in Bovina, Mississippi. Which is a good eight hours away. Our road captains made sure the route is easy and clear all the way through for both clubs.

I jump out of bed, shower, piss a flood and brush my teeth. I put on my standard everyday clothes, black tee shirt, black jeans, black socks, black biker boots and of course my cut. I pack my shit, throw out a group message and turn in the key to my room at the front desk of the hotel.

After about ten minutes, both of the MC members are ready to head out. Storm gives me a nod, but doesn't speak a word to me. She's cold and distant, back to business as usual. Well, damn. I fucked up with her yet again and didn't realize it.

I jump on my bike and take off following Price, watching as Storm and Chyna fly by me. Well, this is turning into a sucky fucking trip after just having one of the best nights of my life. I let the lull of the road calm me and the scenery take me away from my thoughts, as we cruise down the highway until our first stop in about five hours at a little town called Hattiesburg in Mississippi.

Chapter 33: Storm

We stopped here in Louisiana to top off our tanks, use the head and to fuel ourselves up. Ace keeps trying to get my attention, but I keep ignoring him like this is first grade and he has a case of the cooties.

I don't know what I'm supposed to say in these situations. It was my first time having consensual sex, and I got chicken and bailed afterward. He probably thinks I'm crazy since I attacked him right after torturing and killing Monster. God, maybe I am crazy. I don't know. I just know I'm nervous that I enjoyed it. I mean I *thoroughly* enjoyed the sex. I can't imagine it being better than that. I can still feel his lips on mine. The way he touched me and the way my body responded to his, just thinking about it has my cheeks burning.

"Prez, you ok?" Chyna asks, bringing me out of my Ace induced fog.

"Uh, yeah I'm good, Chyna girl." I take a sip of my bottled water and climb on to my bike.

We have about four more hours until we make it to the next hotel and the day's already getting hot. I round the girls up and we get ready to head out and back on the road. First though, I send Ace a text.

Me: Sorry, for bailing. Dinner is on me at the next stop.

Ace: Looking forward to it.

He glances at me and gives me a wink before he places his phone in his pocket.

Another four hours to think about what I'm going to say to him over dinner tonight.

Chapter 34: Ace

I am fucking tired. The trip was long and I want a hot shower, food and to talk to Storm. We pull into a small motel that looks sketchy as fuck. It has a Bate's Motel vibe to it, but I've stayed at clubhouses worse than this place.

The room is small with a bed, dresser, nightstand, and a television. I turn on the TV for some background noise and strip my clothes off. I'm dying to feel the water of a nice hot shower and hoping it will relax my muscles. Don't get me wrong, I fucking love riding, but long trips can make your ass and thighs sore.

The shower really does its job, I feel like a new man. After brushing my teeth and combing my hair I put on a clean pair of jeans and a black tee shirt. I spray some Tom Ford Tobacco Vanille cologne on and pull out my phone.

Me: Ready when you are, Sweetcheeks.

Storm: Don't ever fucking call me that again.

Me: Okay, how about Cupcake?

Storm: Do you want to move up on the vengeance list asshole? Cause I can cut your throat right now.

Me: Come on Storm, give me a break. How about Babydoll?

Storm: Not throat cutting bad, but still not the best. I'm ready, do you want to go find a place in this podunk town or want to order a pizza?

Me: Your choice whatever you want. I'll think of a better pet name.

Storm: Pizza, be there in 5. Call it in .

I look up pizza places near me on Google and find a place that delivers and orders us pizza and breadsticks too.

I just finish ordering when I hear a knock at my door. Storm is wearing a white cami shirt with no bra. Her nipples are poking through and she's wearing a pair of tiny blue shorts that almost look like panties. I stand at the door ogling her until she pushes me out of her way and climbs on my bed. Fuck that woman is so sexy.

"I would have worn more, but it's late and it's not like you haven't seen all of my body." She nonchalantly flips channels on the television.

"I don't mind, fucking believe that sugar tits. You are one fine woman," I remark, knowing the pet name would more than likely get me stabbed.

"You're about to get your tongue cut out so you can't talk," She replies, pulling out a knife. I have no idea where she had it hidden in her lack of clothes.

"Fuck, Storm, you can't do that. You would miss my tongue lapping up that perfect cunt of yours too much." I cross my arms over my chest and smirk at her.

"Well, at least you're good for one thing." She peers at me with a serious look on her face.

"Sex," I state, with a smug expression.

"No. Annoying the fuck out of me," She replies, and starts watching the show on the television.

Chapter 35: Storm

After the pizza is gone and breadsticks are demolished I sink into Ace's bed. I wasn't planning on staying, I just want to end the silence and uncomfortable space that's between us. He gets into bed and lays on his side so that we are facing each other. He's so close I can smell garlic on his breath. We really should brush our teeth, but I'm tired. Sleep has been a distant friend of mine for awhile now and the long bike trip has worn me out and the fact that my stomach is full makes me want to sleep like I'm a baby.

"Your breath smells like garlic and hot garbage," I say, as I turn over in bed.

He starts blowing his hot breath on me and laughing.

"You love it," he replies, trying to blow his nasty pizza breath in my face.

"Stop, dumb ass, you're gross." I try covering my head up, but I'm not quick enough. He grabs me around my stomach and pulls me close to him and then begins to tickle me.

I'm very fucking ticklish. I'm laughing, begging him to stop, but he somehow manages to move me so I'm laying flat on my back and he is over me. He moves really close to my face, so close his lips barely touch mine and if I only move my head up a little bit I'd be able to feel his lips on mine.

The room stills as we gaze each other in the eyes and then he kisses my lips softly. When he removes his lips from mine, he blows his nasty breath in my face again. He cracks up laughing as I fight his hold on me.

When he lets go of my arms, I smack him and go to the bathroom, realizing that my breath probably smells as disgusting as his so I definitely need to do something about it. There's an unopened hotel toothbrush and toothpaste left for guests. I use it since mine is in my hotel room. I brush my teeth not letting the intimacy of that short second of our eyes meeting mean anything. After I rinse my mouth out, Ace comes to the bathroom door.

"Guess I need to brush mine too. I missed out on what could've been a hot sexy moment because my breath stinks like hot garbage." He laughs and puts toothpaste on his toothbrush. I walk back into the bedroom, crawl in his bed, and I'm asleep before he returns.

Chapter 36: Ace

"**P**rez, Dusty has been spotted at a store where he frequently shops. He doesn't wear the Murder of Crows patch anymore," Cash says, as he peers at his phone. Cash, like his twin brother, Price, is a big ol' boy. He's extraordinarily smart and good with numbers, he was going to college as an economics major but dropped out to work for the MC full time. He and his brother are identical besides the ink, Price's scar and Cash's eyes. One is blue and the other is brown. Cash is the MC's treasurer. He's in charge of keeping up with the books on all the club's businesses, legal or not. He also likes to fight at the underground fighting ring. "Supposedly, the North Carolina Chapter sliced off his brand and removed his cut almost twelve years ago. He is no longer a crow."

"What did he do in Astro's territory?" Astro is the president of the Murder of Crows in that area and he's a mean son of a bitch too.

"Well, a friend of mine informs me he was caught fucking the Vice presidents ol' lady without permission." Cash still studies his phone.

"They should've killed him," I say, as I wipe sweat from my brow. "It's all good. Now, Storm is gonna take the trash out. Must be why he's in Mississippi. Gator, the president of Murder of Crows Louisiana Chapter must not know that he's in the area."

"What's our plan?" asks Chyna, stepping out from behind Zeus.

"We are going to have a few of us stake-out the store and give us a heads up when he's been spotted. Then we can follow him to his house," Cash says, looking at Chyna then Storm. "How does that sound to you?"

"It could get messy at his house. We have to be careful in case he is living with someone. We don't kill innocent people," She says, gazing at me. "If they can follow him home and make sure it's clear then I'm fine with it, but this one I want to play with a little." A mischievous smile forms across her face. She went from Doctor Quinzel to Harley Quinn in ten seconds and I know that Dusty's death is going to be not only bloody but painful.

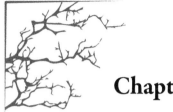

Chapter 37: Storm

As I survey through the binoculars at Dusty's falling down shack, I freeze remembering him from the night I was raped. He was the fucker who cut me and was brutal when he took me, smiling when I tried to get away. This fucker knew he hurt me, and liked it. I'm going to make him hurt and I'm going to love it. I went to the hunting store a few towns over just for my surprise for Dusty.

"I'm going to go and knock on his door and when he opens I'm going to give him the rules to our game," I tell Ace and Chyna. "Make sure he doesn't get far from me. I doubt he will, but just in case." I get my bow ready, check my nine millimeter, and strap on my knife.

"Game on, motherfucker," I snarl, as I walk up to the little run down shack in the middle of nowhere. "Time to go hunting."

I bang on the peeling paint for the front door. The flecks from when I knocked fall like scattered ashes at my feet as I wait for him to answer the door.

The hinges screech and I'm meeting with a skeptical, pursed lipped rapist that plays as though fate would never catch up to him until I came along. "Who the..." he starts to say, as I put my knife up to his neck.

"I'm going to slit your throat if you make one move I don't like. First, I want you to remove any weapons you have on you." I push him back, walking us further into the house. "Then I'm going to explain the rules to a game you and I are going to play. You like games right?" He nods his head. "Good, now I'm going to ask you a few questions and I want honest answers. If you lie to me you'll die right now, do you understand?"

He nods his head again.

"Do you remember who I am?" Again, he nods, but this time sweat beads from his forehead, dripping down and pooling on my blade.

My lips pull in disgust at the nasty fuck. "You raped me and hurt me and you smiled like a kid in a candy store, *Dusty*. You degraded *me* and broke *me* and that made *you* happy." I grit my teeth, restraining myself from slitting his throat right here and now. "You know you deserve everything that's coming to you right?"

He doesn't move his head at all. "I *said* you deserve to die for what you did to me and probably other girls as well, right?" Annoyed that I have to repeat myself, I knick his neck and a drop of blood runs down his chest.

He tries to pull away from me, but I grip the nap of his neck and aim the sharp point toward his eyeball. "You're gonna die tonight, but I'm going to give you what you didn't give me."

"What's that?" he asks in a shaky voice.

I can't help the way a smile threatens to tug at my lips. He's already scared of me and I love it. "I'm going to give you a *running* chance." I take my free hand, check his pockets, and throw his phone at the wall. I let that smile I've been suppressing bloom into a full on manic grin. "Then I'm going to hunt you down and kill you."

I take my gun out and point it at him. "Now take off all your weapons."

"I ain't got none," he says, as I walk a few feet away.

"Then run. Open the door and run like the scared little rabbit you are." I laugh hysterically, pointing the gun at him., but he leaps forward, catching me off guard. He swings a knife hitting my shoulder. The searing pain doesn't register at first. Only running on adrenaline and acting on instinct, I shoot him in the foot.

"You fucking dumb bastard! You're so fucking dead!" I scream, staring down at him where he's fallen, clutching his injured foot. "You better run! You have a one minute head start then I'm going to use your ass as target practice." He scrambles, heading out the door, limping as fast as he can.

Warm liquid runs down my arm from where he sliced me with his knife. It's bleeding profusely, but thankfully, the adrenaline pumping through my veins seems to dull the pain for now. *The memory of him threatening to use the blade to fuck me, runs through my mind.* I tear a piece of my shirt and tie it around my arm making a bandage. I get my bow ready and nock my arrow as I watch him go through the woods.

The woods around his house are dense and the bed of the forest floor is covered in dead leaves. I follow behind him, quietly to not give him any indication of where I am. Since I shot him in the foot, he doesn't have the advantage of suppressing the sound of his steps like I do. He peeks his head out from behind a tree and I shoot, hitting the trunk where he's hiding.

"You crazy cunt! I'mma cut your tits off and shove 'em down your throat," he snarls, as he moves deeper into the woods.

The horrible scent of his breath as he holds me down, I try to scream, my voice a shout into the void. I can't move as he brings the knife to me, raking it along my flesh as he laughs manically.

"How do you plan on doing that? You're a fucking pedophile rapist that's running from a woman on a shot foot. You ain't gonna do shit."

There's a loud pop and wood chips rain down on the spot where I'm crouched.. Multiple shots ricochet on the trees around. Fuck, he must have weapons hidden out here. I pull out my phone and quickly send a text to Ace. At least if something happens to me then they will be prepared.

The feeling of the blade slicing through my stomach, feeling the pain, but unable to do anything to stop him. His long tongue lapping up the blood as he laughs manically over me. Being helpless, unable to keep him from hurting me.

I patrol deeper, slinking between the trees and heavily cloaked areas until I see a flash of blue. He thinks he's hiding but he's not. He's like a white rabbit hiding amongst the dark trees. I nock my arrow and squint my eye, aiming for the kill. Centering myself, I take a deep breath and let it go.

"AHHH, you fucking bitch." He groans in agony, crying like a wounded animal.

I pump my fist at my side, rejoicing in my victory. "Come on out, you cocksucker and I'll give you a quick death by shooting your brains out?"

"Fuck you!" he seethes, scampering away.

I head in the direction his voice comes from and laugh as I watch him weaving and bobbing, dodging my aim amongst the trees. It's so cute to watch him run like he has a chance. The further we journey the canopy above grows more dense, snuffing out what little light the moon provides. The sounds of the forest surrounds me. I sit still hiding beside a big log, waiting and listening for any footprints or sounds that he may be near.

After a few moments of silence, he must get antsy and starts running from tree to tree. He really has burned up his brain cells over the years if he thinks he can outrun me. He was better off hiding, but he probably also knows that I won't give up until he's dead. His feet crunch over fallen leaves on the forest floor, but I'll let him fall into a false sense of security before I catch him.

He's hobbling from tree to tree, but this time he retraces our path. I wait until the perfect moment when he passes me. I nock my bow and aim.

A scream that should never come from a grown man's lips, pierces the air and my lips pull in a devious smile. I shouldn't enjoy this as much as I am but the hollow thumb of the earth as he falls to his side is like a symphony I want to play over and over again. It's something I could fall asleep peacefully to.

I meander and skip with my bow over my shoulder to him. The moonlight captures the shine of tears that rim his lower lids.

"Ahhh." I breathe out in utter bliss as I place my boot on the hand that's still clutching the gun with his last thread of hope. Then I shoot an arrow into his palm which keeps it in place.

"Looks like this cunts got you now," I mock. "So, I did my research before I decided to play our game." I crouch down, looking him in the eye and use my bow to prop myself up nonchalantly. "Turns out a person can survive being hit with an arrow ten or more times, without bleeding to death. Especially if you don't hit any main arteries." My gaze scans his body for dramatic effect and he pisses his pants. I chuckle. "Let's see how long it takes *you*."

"No, I'll do anything you want. I'll tell you everything, just please, don't kill me!" Dusty, begs for his life. Terror fills his eyes as the realization hits him that he isn't going to make it out of these woods alive.

The tears that stream down his cheeks and trepidation that trembles through his entire body makes me happy. I love the fear in his eyes as I load my bow. The cord is drawn tight before the arrow snaps the short distance to his arms, legs, ears, and balls. He cries as I shoot him over and over again. The color in his face pales in the moonlight as life drains out of him slowly with each shot. "Looks like *seventeen*." That last word spews like acid from my mouth before I shoot my last arrow into Dusty's black heart.

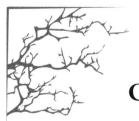

Chapter 38: Ace

When I reach Storm, she's kneeling on the ground just a few feet away from Dusty's body. She really did a number on him. His body looks kind of like a pin-head porcupine covered in arrows. *My storm* brought the thunder and lighting strikes down on him in her mission of retribution.

It's raining now and water droplets drip down from her loose strands that hang down in front of her face. She's a wet mess sitting on the floor of the forest. I grab her by the waist and lift her up, clutching her to me with her head on my chest. I know that this vengeance kill is different from the last, because she lets me hold her and she sinks into my touch. This one has taken a toll on her, mentally. I find Chyna coming towards us and tell her to notify the team, so that they can find Dusty and begin the clean up. Instead of arguing that I wasn't her President, she nods her head, and I can only guess it's because she sees Storm curled up in my arms. Storm's girls' love and respect her. That says alot about the sisterhood that Storm has with them.

I carry Storm back to where our bikes are and hold onto her. She eventually loosens her grip and stares up at me.

"Three more to go," I say, wanting to kiss away her pain. I won't though, not unless she makes the first move.

"Three more," She responds, sitting up and digging for a bottle of water out of the pannier on the side of her motorcycle.

She gulps down the water in a haste and then does something on her phone.

A few minutes later, Siren and a few others come out of the woods.

"They are taking care of the body. We also wiped down his shack so no trace of entry can be found," Zeus says, as he walks back to his bike. "Is she good?" He nods toward Storm.

"I'm good," Storm replies, "Siren, tell the girls to come in. The men have clean up. We need to get back to the motel. I need a room. We have to go back home and check on my girls' there. Seems like they have been having problems while we've been away."

"What kind of problems?" I cross my arms in front of my chest. "My guys can help."

"I'll fill you in later," She says, as she starts her bike. The girls' join her in unison and take off back toward the motel.

Zeus glances at me and a smirk comes across his face. "Do ya think she's gonna take you out, Prez?"

"I don't know, but if she decides that she wants vengeance on my father by taking my life. You are to make sure no one retaliates. Do you understand? If one finger is laid on her by one of our brothers then that's one less brother, got it?" I point a finger at him to give more emphasis on my words. His eyes soften and I know he understands what I'm getting at. My father was a piece of shit and I *am* the sins of my father. "We owe her this. I owe her this," I say, as we climb on our bikes, message the rest of the guys to go back to the motel as soon as they are done and leave Dusty's shack of squalor.

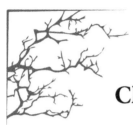

Chapter 39: Chyna

When we arrive back at the motel, I can tell Storm is in a dark place. I rub my hand over my chest to dull the pain that's throbbing there. I'm not one to break down for anyone ever, but when it comes to Storm my heart aches for what she's been through. With Storm's arm over my shoulder, I help her room to her room and get her to the bathroom. That's what she needs right now, a hot shower makes everyone feel a little better at least for the moment. She needs more than that to help with black cloud over her head, but this is what I can do for her right now. I turn on the hot water and begin undressing my President, my best friend, my *sister*. I've seen her scars before, the one that runs across her stomach and the ones on her thighs. I'm probably one of the very few that has. Storm notices me looking at them and peers up at me.

"He's the one who did them," She says, as she steps into the tub. "As I was shooting him, I had flashbacks, slimmers of memory. He was the most violent of them. He would cut me then smile as he licked up my blood. How fucked up is that?"

"He can't hurt you or anyone again. You made sure of that," I reassure before leaving to grab her something to sleep in out of her bag, and lay it on the sink.

Storm is my best friend. She's more than just the leader of an all women's motorcycle club. Storm is kind, giving, and strong. She's helped me at a time when I was hopeless and didn't have anything, not even the will to live. The night she found me I had run away from my abusive husband. I was living on the streets and became a sex worker so I could buy food and things I needed to get by. Storm took me in. She gave me a place to call home and a family of equally messed up sisters and vowed to me that I'd never suffer at the hands of another man ever again. I soon realized that I loved working out, lifting weights and boxing. I was also good at it. I bulked up and my muscles developed. I became stronger in all ways, both mentally and physically.

I turn on the television and sit in the chair in her room. I'm determined to stay and to be here for her until she asks me to leave.

A LIGHT TOUCH ON MY arm Jars me awake. The anchor on TV gabbers on about the weather forecast for the week to come. I glance up after blinking away the haze of sleep to meet brown eyes with a midnight halo.

"Chyna, why don't you go on to your room?" Storm asks. Her hand is still on my forearm. I must've fallen asleep in the chair.

"Are you sure boss? I can sleep in here tonight if you need me too."

"I'm okay, Chyna girl. I'm going to bed myself." She gazes at me as she sits on her bed.

Her eyes are rimmed with redness which is probably from crying in the shower.. I have to fight the urge to argue with her and stand to give her a hug. She even wraps her arms around me which is an odd show of affection from her. I only wanted to give something, not expecting anything in return.

"If you need me I'm just a text away," I whisper into her damp hair.

She nods and I release her turning toward the door. I twist the handle to leave and go to my hotel room, but I'm met with Ace holding his fist up in mid knock.

"Prez, you have company," I call over my shoulder.

I stand in the doorway for a moment and peer at him. "Take care of our girl."

"Always."

I move out of his way and let him enter the room, before closing the door behind me. He had better take care of her, or he'll quickly realize that black eye I gave him was only a miniscule of my actual strength.

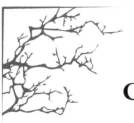

Chapter 40: Ace

There's a soft click as the door closes behind me. I don't miss the hidden threat in Chyna's words. Knowing her, she'll make good on her promise. I take a few steps into Storm's room. She's laying in the bed and she looks so small. Her dark hair halos her head in wet gnarled strands. . I saunter over to the counter in the bathroom and pick up the blow dryer and her brush. With all her hair appliances and tools in my arms, I stand by the bed in front of her.

"Scoot up and let me behind you." I plug up the hair dryer in the outlet beside the bed.

Without saying anything, she moves up on the bed so that I can get behind her. The smell of her coconut shampoo fills the air, as I blow dry and brush out her long locks of brown hair flowing down her back until it's silky smooth. I kiss the top of her head and she lays back onto me.

"Will you just hold me Talon?" she whispers, snuggling up farther into me.

I don't comment on her calling me by my birth name. Instead, I pull her to me as if she's a child, sitting sideways on my lap, letting her legs dangle to the side with her head tucked under my chin. I cover us up with the comforter and I hold her like that until her breathing slows. A light snore escapes her lips and I know my girl is off into dreamland. My body warms with adoration for this woman and I'll never let her go again. I us down and pull her close to me. Her body spooning with mine like it was made for me and I hold her close breathing in her coconut shampoo until I fall asleep.

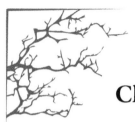

Chapter 41: Storm

"It's gone. The whole clubhouse." That's the situation I'm dealing with at the moment. "We have a few people on video, but you can't really see their faces. I ran the video through software, but it's not showing anything. What do you want us to do, Prez?" Bear's pissed off and the sadness in her voice is upsetting.

"Is everyone safe? Do y'all have a place to stay? Take money out of the books for it. Also, go back and empty the safe. Let me know where you set everyone up and we'll head back to Heron. Just make them aware that we'll have some members of the Crows in tow." I start to get dressed. "I need you to get everyone settled and then we'll figure this shit out. Thanks, Bear. Love ya." I hang up the phone before putting on my cut and my boots, time to head back to California.

"Fuck! We don't have any issues with other motorcycle clubs, so who the hell would've torched the club?" I'm thinking out loud as my phone goes off with a message. It's pictures of two guys in black hoodies, their faces covered by skeleton masks. I scan the pictures and see nothing that can be used to identify them with or their club. I place my phone in my pocket and grab my brush to throw my hair up in a ponytail.

Once my bags are packed, I'm ready to head to California. I open the door to the bright sun that warms my face and arms and breath in the summer air. *We got this. Everything will be okay.* My steps beat against the asphalt as I walk toward the line of bikes. My stomach sinks when I notice Chyna sitting on a bench. Her muscular arms are crossed and her head is bowed. The closer I get the more her facial expression grows more prominent. Her brows are bunched in a look of pure distress, so I take the seat beside her.

"What the fuck we gonna do Prez? We have no home. We have nothing."

"Chyna, we'll be okay. We are strong, smart, kick ass, bitches. No one's gonna keep us down. We'll find out who did this and we'll be like a mother fucking Phoenix rising from the ashes." I put my arm around her shoulders. "Besides, I think getting out of California altogether sounds like a good plan."

"It would probably be for the best, Prez. I think that this could be a sign that we need to start a new chapter in our lives."

"Go get the girls. It's time to head out," I say, patting her shoulder.

"On it, boss." She nods her head once and heads back into the hotel.

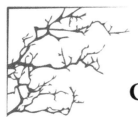

Chapter 42: Ace

I'm so fucking worried. I'm worried about what we'll walk into when we arrive at Storm's clubhouse and worried about finding Jaxx, one of the rapists on Storm's vengeance list. If I'm honest, I'm worried about whether or not Storm is going to put a bullet in my brain for the sins of my father.

The best thing about long bike rides is when you get to enjoy the nice weather. We ride all day, until our tanks and our energy levels are running low. The motel we decide to stay at for the night is old and dingy. It looks worse than the last. The paint is peeling, there's wood over some of the windows in different rooms. I bet they even have vermin. It would be no surprise to me if there are bedbugs, rats, or roaches, but at least it is somewhere to stay for the night.

"Want to share a room?" I smirk at Storm, really wanting her in my arms and my dick sheathed in her warm tight cunt tonight.

"Nope, I'm tired, big boy." She pats my chest. "You better use Susie Palmer tonight." Then she clips my shoulder playfully as she flings open the motel office door and walks in.

The motel's office is just as ragged as the outside and the old woman running the front desk coughs up a lung. I pull my lips back in a grimace and have to cough into my own fist to cover it. She appears cachectic as if she's about to keel over at any time.

We get enough rooms for everyone and pass out the room keys out front. After the room keys are given out, I walk Storm to her room. She gives me a hug and I hold her to me briefly.

"Goodnight," she says, before pulling away from me and closing the rickety door in my face.

My steps are heavy and my shoulders are slouched as my head hangs to my chest. I'm in a pissy mood as I clomp up the breezeway to my hotel room. I unlock the door to find a tiny, 80's style room that reeks of stale cigarettes which only adds to my shitty disposition. Ugly paintings hang on the walls, the bedspread looks like it is made from wool. That's going to be scratchy. I pull it and the sheet off to check for bedbugs. Hallelujah! It's clean, which is a fucking miracle. The small table that resides in the corner, has multiple burns from cigarettes and the television that rests on an old chest of drawers is adorned with a set of rabbit ears. I bet it can't pick up anything, but local channels. Fuck it! A shower and sleep, that's all I need. I replace the sheet and quilt back on the bed.

I peel off all my clothes and turn on the hot water, it takes a few minutes before it heats up and I step inside. I'm tired, stressed and to be honest I need a little release. Here I am again with my fist wrapped around my shaft with the thought of Storm's chocolate brown eyes. I picture her on her knees in the shower with me. Her pretty luscious lips are open and waiting for me. I palm my long, thick cock and stroke it, making myself hard.

"You want my cock don't you?" I say, to my imaginary vision of Storm. She nods her head and peeks up at me. The water from the shower runs down her face as she opens her mouth wider. Her tongue licks my tip and I just know her mouth on me would feel *so* damn good. I stroke a little harder as my imaginary Storm takes me in all the way.

"That's it baby, you're such a good cocksucker," I groan, as I feel her warm mouth and her juicy lips wrap around my length.

I use my other hand to play with my balls as I wrap my hand harder around my dick, picturing fucking Storm's mouth. In no time, my balls tighten up and I grunt. My come spraying all over the shower wall. The release was good, but fucking my Storm would've been so much better. I scrub myself off, rinse off, and brush my teeth. Sad that I have to hop into my bed all alone.

Chapter 43: Storm

FUCK! *Fuck! Fuck!* I cuss out loud as we pull up in front of what used to be the Daughters of Doom Motorcycle Club house. There's nothing left but stray metal and a pile of fucking ashes. My whole dream, my home, my sister's home is gone. My chest is constricted with a sense of overwhelming despair. I'd cry, but I have to be strong for my girls'. I embrace Bear in a tight hug as she comes running up to me.

"We savaged all we could, Prez, but there wasn't much left. Most of the girls' got their bikes out as the building went up in flames." She unwraps her long arms from around my neck and steps back.

"Fuck, Bear, I should've been here. I should've been the one here for y'all." I examine what's left of our home. Our hopes and dreams blow away in small indeservable pieces in the wind..

"Round all the girls' up and we'll meet at the city park in an hour. We need to see what we're going to do and if we should rebuild here or maybe move our club closer to Kentucky," I say to Chyna, as she begins to look through a pile of ashes. "I don't think anyone is keen on staying in California and maybe a slow paced style might be good for us, regardless I need to see my sister's."

Chyna nods her dark head and pulls out her phone. I turn around and see Ace and the guys standing by their bikes. All of them are wearing sullen looks. I think they are bad for us, pity us even. They, I'm sure, are glad it wasn't them this happened to.

I trek over to Ace's group. All of them open their mouths as if they're ready to say something, but I hold my hand up to stop them. I'm not looking for their condolences. "Look, we're having church at the local park. Y'all are more than welcome to come, but it's not your place to say anything. So, your opinions are to be kept to yourself."

I climb onto my bike and start my beauty up. The guilt for not being here for my sisters eats away at me, making my stomach burn, and tears come to my eyes from all we've lost. I'll be damned, if anyone will see me cry. Ace is the first and only one to bear witness to that. I have to be strong for my girls. They're my sisters, my family, and all that I have left.

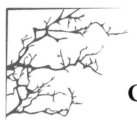

Chapter 44: Ace

The city park is a small play area for kids accompanied by a picnic area that is covered for people to bbq and celebrations. I'm sure it is intimidating to civilians who have to walk by big burly biker guys and hot, scantily clad chicks all gathering at the park like some kind of fucked up family reunion. The ladies, who I assume all make up Storm's council, are at the head of the picnic table while my brothers, who are here, stand around as church begins.

I love watching her as she takes charge. There's no sign on her face that she's broken, but I know it though. I can read it in her big brown eyes. As soon as she received the call that her clubhouse was torched, flames were in her eyes and a devouring look of sadness overcame her. I felt sorry for her, but I also wanted to fuck her pain away. It's a juxtaposition of epic proportion. I've done nothing, but sit back and hope she would seek comfort in my arms, but she hasn't though. I have to discern that the Kelsey that I remembered from our childhood no longer exists. When Kelsey needed me, I was her protector, I gave her strength. Storm on the other hand is strong all on her own. She needs no one, but wants those she cares about, mainly, her chosen family of vigilant sisters close.

Storm is a force of nature, a hurricane that sucks up all around her leaving them in a beautiful fucked up mess. As I watch her on this hot, sun-shiny day gear up her club for a fight, I know that I love her. I always have. The little girl she was and the beautiful fierce woman she is today, I will always love her. Now, I have to find a way to get her to love me back. The first thing I have to do is find out who has done this to her clubhouse, to her family and make them fucking pay.

The guys all sit back quietly, taking in all the information that Storm's girl, Bear gives about what happened that night and showing everyone a video of two hooded guys throwing molotov cocktails and bailing. The guy's faces were covered by skeleton masks or balaclavas, with black hoodies, black pants and nothing else to identify who they are. Software showed the guys to be about 6'5 and 6'2 in height, about two hundred twenty pounds both hefty guys, but as I look closely at the hand of the tallest guy, part of a tattoo skull can be seen and I know exactly who the mystery arsonist is.

Abbadon. Abbadon used to be my father's grim reaper when he was president of the Crows. He's a heartless bastard who will kill anything, a total fucking psychopath. Storm has no idea what kind of demon truly has started war with her and I'm guessing it has everything to do with all his buddies suddenly disappearing. *Fuck!*

Chapter 45: Storm

I pound on Ace's door. I don't know why I came here. After having church at the park, I came back to the hotel, took a hot shower, and fell asleep for hours afterwards. When I woke up, I had an immediate need to be near Ace. So here I am banging on his door at one in the morning.

"Coming!" A groggy voice calls, right before Ace opens the door. His black hair is tousled and black boxers ride low on his hips. "Storm." My name barely manages to escape his lips before I pull him, crashing my mouth to his.

He growls before putting his arms around me and lifting me up so my legs wrap around his waist. Ace removes my shirt quickly. The door scarcely shuts before we are giving the parking lot a show. He uses his tongue and licks against my lips, coaxing them open until I'm inviting him to kiss me deeper.

He sits on the bed with me on his lap, and I waste no time slipping my hand past the latex band of his boxers. He doesn't stop me as I take his long, thick, hard cock out. His lips never leave mine. The only reaction I get are his tightening abs that flex at my light touch. I wrap my hand around his hard length, pumping him.

"I want you inside me," I pant a mere centimeter from his lips.

He nodes and I pull back to see the lust consuming his eyes. His lips are red, begging for me to bite them. I give him a quick nip with my teeth, pulling his lip away and releasing it with a pop. The reaction he gives is feral and I jump off his lap, pushing his boxers down farther and unbuttoning my jeans. It's as if we're hungry and starving for touch with how quickly we remove our clothes. We take each other in, our chests heaving then lays back on the bed.

"Come take what you want, Dollface. Use me, fuck me." He licks the cut I've made on his lip as his eyes consume every inch of me. "It's yours. You can do what you want to me."

He grabs my hips as I climb up on top of him. My wet, slick cunt hovers just above his cock. I grab him, lining his cock up with my entrance and I take him to the hilt.

"Fuck, Storm, I love the way your needy pussy takes all of me." I lean over to kiss him as I move my hips, riding him, feeling him deep inside me.

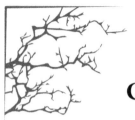

Chapter 46: Ace

I'm not going to lie. Seeing Storm at my door was a huge surprise and the way she practically attacked me was an even bigger shock. Right now, she is riding my cock and fucking herself like it's Dooms day and this is the last sex she'll ever get. I don't mind her using my body to make herself feel better. I know that's what she's doing. I'm her release, her sexual stress ball and that's why I'm letting her be in control. Well that and the fact that she's a sexual fiend. It's a bonus for me that in this position her tits are at just the right angle to watch them bouncing up and down as she takes my cock. I run my hand up her stomach, cupping her breast, relishing in the softness of her skin against my callous palms. Her nipples are taut and begging for my attention so I pinch them and pull them. The action causes her to whine in pleasure. Her brows knit together and her jaw grows slack as I play with them and I glide my other hand to rub her swollen desperate clit.

"That's it baby, show me who this dick belongs to," I say, as I move my hips up and slam into her. She moans my name, scratching my chest with her nails. "Mark me baby, do what you want to me," I growl, pounding up into her. Her pussy tightens, squeezing my cock in a vice grip as she chases her orgasm.

I flip our bodies, taking control of the situation. Storm's eyes roll to the back of her head as I thrust into her deeper. Electricity races down my spine and settles heavy in my lower spine. Our skins slap together like a beat to a song. I grip her ankle, lifting it to my shoulder, so I can watch as her hungry pussy takes me in. My balls tighten at the sight of us, loving how our bodies seem to be made for each other. She looks up at me, her mouth forming an O as she lets out a guttural moan of pleasure. Her cunt drips with her release, pulsing around my length. My thrusts grow frantic. That pressure building to a crescendo in our sweet symphony of flesh. A few more thrusts into her and the stars are bursting in my vision. I pump my own release filling her up with my come.

I brace myself using my forearms to hover over her so I don't put too much weight on her chest and bring my lips to her, kissing her forehead.

"Thanks, I needed that," she whispers, patting my shoulder as if to distance herself and to get me off of her. I lay beside her and gather her to me, holding her in my arms.

"You can talk to me, you know," I say against her hair as I hold her. "I won't tell anyone."

"I know." She pushes herself from me and goes into the bathroom. I hear the shower water running and my feet lead before my brain does.

The rings holding the plastic curtain click as I pull it back and step inside the warm spray. She gazes up at me. Her brown eyes are glassy with unshed tears. I run my thumb over her bottom lip and she sucks the tip of my finger. Her hand grazes down my body as she takes my shaft into her small hand, pumping me gently at first and then quicker. I pop my thumb out of her mouth and she falls to her knees.

She's still gazing up at me and I'm hit with one of my previous fantasies. The water cascades down my body like a waterfall soaking her. When she inches closer to my cock, her tongue darts out licking up the precome that is beading at the slit. I'm ready to go for round two with her. I place my hand on the back of her head, as she opens her mouth. My abs flex with anticipation. She cups her tongue and I lay my shaft on her hot, wet tongue.

"I've fantasized about you on your knees for me, but the reality is so much better," I growl, rubbing my cock against her tongue before slapping it.

I'm only teasing myself with this, but it's worth every agonizing minute. Her lips wrap around me and her cheeks hollow out, sucking me into her warm waiting mouth. She teases my head, licking around it before taking me all the way to the back of her throat. That intense weight in my spine builds again with delicious torment. I pull her closer to me, thrusting into her mouth.

She allows me to pump into her while looking up at me. "How far can you take me, cupcake?"

There's a fire in her eyes as I use the nickname she didn't like before and it causes a chuckle to rubble in my chest. I take her head and push her down on my cock. Her throat closes, clenching around the head. Her eyes begin to water so I pull her off, but she is only off of me for a second. An inferno is blazing in her gaze before taking me down again. This time though she's taking it as a challenge and my dick is being squeezed as she chokes me down. To top it all off, she fucking moans. The vibrations go straight to my balls.

"Oh, Fuck!" A savage groan is ripped from my throat as the woman at my feet sucks the soul from my body.

I love the feel of her mouth on me. My girthiness not stopping how deep she takes me down. When she sticks her finger in my ass, I thrust my hips into her harder, causing her to gag. I ease out of her and back in. She works me faster, and harder. Shocks pulsate down my spine, and my balls tighten when I climax. I pull out of her and she waits, peering up at me with her tongue sticking out. I squirt her mouth full, watching as it runs down her mouth and onto her tits.

She swallows me down with a devious smirk on her lips and I help her back up, taking her lips with mine, tasting the saltiness of my come. "Who's a cupcake? I'm pretty sure you're the one with a surplus of icing on demand."

"You bring it out of me," I say with a shrug.

Not wanting to push her any further by saying she's the one covered in it. Instead, I turn her around, grab the shampoo and pour some into my hand. I lather up her hair and then do the same with the conditioner. I take a cloth and clean her. Once I'm sure she's thoroughly taken care of, I wash myself. When we are all clean, I dry her off and carry her to my bed where she drifts off to sleep. I snuggle her close to me and hold her.

"I love you, Kelsey," I whisper, before I close my eyes and fall asleep, too.

"MURPHY, I NEED YOU and Price to have Techie to check any CCTV's the city of Heron may have for anything that may lead to Abbadon's hideout. That includes any places close to the D.O.D's clubhouse. We need a license plate or something. Those fuckers are around here somewhere and we need to find them before they strike again," I whisper into my phone. Storm is still asleep, because I don't want her to know that I'm planning on finding this guy for her.

"I'll get back to ya, Prez, if we find anything." There's a click from the other line as Murphy hangs up the phone.

I kiss Storm's forehead which causes her to moan in her sleep. "I'm going to head to the bakery down the street to get us some breakfast."

"Maple bacon doughnut and orange juice," She murmurs, as she turns over and covers her head.

"Will do, Dollbaby," I say, putting on my cut. Thankfully, she doesn't hear that or I'd get more than a little earth shattering blow job from her this morning.

Chapter 47: Storm

"Hello." I stretch and yawn as I answer the phone.

"Listen here you fucking cunt," the deep voice says, after I pick up the phone. "I have Ace and if you ever want to see this sorry excuse for a motorcycle club president alive again, you'll do what I say."

"Who is this?" I ask, sitting up straighter in bed and hitting the voice record button on my phone, so I can record what's being said.

"Are you dumb, bitch? I said listen."The man clears his throat and I can hear muffled noises as he tells someone to shut up. "You will come alone to the abandoned warehouse at the industrial park. If we see or even get a whiff of one of your slut bitches, I'll slit this pussy motherfucker's throat. You have one hour." The phone goes dead. I jump out of bed dialing Zeus' number, and throwing on my clothes.

"Zeus, bring everyone to my room, Ace is fucked and we need a plan," I command, hanging up the phone and brushing my hair to throw it up in a Ponytail.

My day has just got bad, and damn it I was really wanting that doughnut and orange juice.

Ten minutes later and with fifty minutes left, my hotel room is full of both club's members'.

"Trace Ace's phone and make sure he's at the warehouse. I don't want to ride into an even bigger trap and he won't even be there," I say, looking at a map of the Heron Industrial Park. "Look there's a dirt road that leads to the back of the park, I need y'all to stay hidden while I go in."

"Fuck that Storm, you can't go in there by yourself," Zeus declares, rubbing his jaw. "I can't let you."

"Zeus, I don't need any of y'alls fucked up "men are tougher than women" cavemen bullshit. I might not be as strong as you but I'm a bad bitch. I'm one of the best shots here. I know how to fight and can shoot you in the heart with an arrow from five hundred feet away, don't fuck with me." I stand up and poke him in the chest. "This is my club, my girls, my family and just because you *men* think because you have a cock *you* rule the world, but not here. Here I'm the motherfucking queen!"

"Okay, tell us what you need us to do." He steps back, holding his hands up.

I give everyone their instructions of how the plan is going to work out. How I'm going to get their President and *my man* back. I think about that for a second, my man, yep, sounds good to me.

After the meeting, I step outside into the sun and climb on to my bike. Hopefully, not for the last time.

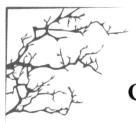

Chapter 48: Ace

"**W**ake up you bastard!" A burn engulfs my cheeks and a resounding smack echoes in my ears. The strike against my face has me jolting awake. *Fuck that stings*, I think to myself as I try to focus on the dipshit snapping his fingers infront of my face. Abbadon.

"Where the hell am I?" I try to speak but my words are jumbled and my mouth feels like it's full of sand.

"Boy, you sure have turned the Crows into a laughing stock. Your dad would roll over in his grave if he could see what you've turned his club into." Abbadon's voice is gravely and deep as though he has smoked a million cigarettes.

"Oh, you mean because we don't rape innocent little girl's anymore," I spit back, at the guy who I remember from my teenage years. He looks the same except his face is older, with wrinkles, his hair is balding, and his clothes are dirty.

"Wait until that sweet thing comes to save your ass. I'm going to do more than rape her. I'm going to gut her from cunt to sternum and I'm going to make you watch as me and my guys fuck every hole in her body. Plus, the ones we make." He coughs and it sounds wet like he's going to hack up a lung.

"You have no fucking clue what shes capable of you rapist piece of shit! She'll rip your balls off and force your buddies to eat them while you watch," I scoff, trying to sit up straighter. "Tough move by the way, ramming my motorcycle off the road, makes you look like you're the ones with a vagina." That comment earns me a punch in the gut and a mouth full of knuckles. I spit out the blood. "Is that the best you got?" I smile, blood pouring out of my lip.

"I'm going to cut out your tongue. You disrespectful little piece of shit." He pulls out a hunting knife and steps closer when all of a sudden one of the guys falls to the floor. Abbadon grabs me and holds a knife to my throat as his friend lays on the wooden floor with an arrow in his heart.

"You are fucked, Abbadon! You think she can't kill you? She already took out all of your pedophile, kid fucking friends and now she's coming after you," I say, as he maneuvers the knife closer to my jugular.

"Show yourself you twat, or imma kill your boyfriend!" A noise comes from behind us, and he turns around giving me enough momentum to head butt him. I fall to my side, working the rope that has me tied to a chair when a gunshot rings throughout the building and Abbadon's other lanky, who I believe is Jaxx, falls to the ground with a bullet in his skull.

"Two more to go," Storm announces, standing over the body of the last man she killed.

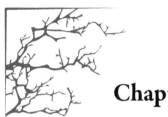

Chapter 49: Storm

I jump down from the rafters as the others come sneaking in from various entry points into the warehouse. The old man has upgraded from a hunting knife and now points a gun at Ace.

"You pull that trigger you cock sucker and I'll torture you for months. You'll cry and beg for relief, but it'll never come," I growl. "You might as well give up, I killed all of your skanky friends. I made them pincushions and flayed them. I've been quite creative if I do say so myself. They were no longer recognizable once I was done with them. It's quite poetic though if you think about it. The first man who touched me was you and you're gonna be the last of my rapists to die."

"You were so tight. I remember it like it was yesterday. Did you enjoy the broken ribs? Prez didn't order the beating, but after all, the club had you. I figured I could do what I wanted to you." A creepy smile comes to his face. He coughs and then spits on Ace. "I know I'm outnumbered, and that I'm going to die today. I'm not dumb, but you'll have to live the rest of your life with what I've done to you and with watching your precious Talon die at your hands." His finger is on the trigger of his gun, pointing at Ace. Chyna sneaks up behind him and grabs his arm, sending the bullet flying hitting Ace in the leg.

Chyna wrestles the gun from him. She holds Abbadon down as Zeus makes his way to help her. Siren rushes to Ace, tearing a strip of fabric from her shirt to try to stop the bleeding in his leg.

"Big mistake, jackass!" I yell, hauling back and hitting him straight in the nose, knocking him out. "You're about to have the worst day of your life."

I PUT THE SMELLING salts under Abbandon's nose causing him to wake up instantly. He's tied to a table that has clear painters plastic over it. The room is a homage to my favorite television show, Dexter. He would be proud of the kill room I've created. All around are the pictures of every victim, whose innocence or life was taken by him. His mouth is duct taped closed, but his mumbling can still be heard.

"Are you trying to beg me not to kill you?" I say, "because it won't work. I've heard enough from you and your vile mouth."

I pull out my eight inch serrated knife and cut a slice out of his cheek. I lift it up and show him the slab of bloody meat. "I think I'm going to skin you alive. After all, that's what kid fuckers and scum deserve." Ace takes a deer skinning knife out of his sheath and hands it to me.

I start with his chest, slowly removing his skin from his muscles in long strips like you would remove the peel from a potato. Abbadon keeps passing out as I skin him. Which reminds me of how I went in and out of consciousness when he was raping me. I have to keep waking him up so he can feel what I'm doing to him. Sooner rather than later he'll stop feeling the pain though, which is too bad.

There's a consistent drip as blood drips onto the tarp covering the floor at my feet. I have to admit, even I'm grossed out a little by the sight of Abbadon's body. I Googled how long someone can stay alive after being flayed and remarkably it said a few days, if they're in a sterile environment. Which I doubt would describe this place with the piles of rat shit, cobwebs and filth hiding in the corners.

I continue with my masterpiece while jamming to the horror band, Ice Nine Kills until I have every single sliver of skin showing from his neck down, besides his penis. I have other plans for his crotch area. I slide my knife between his legs and slice off his ballsack and penis.

Then I grab a handful of white crystals and shove salt into the wound. His eyes fly open with renewed strength and his gut curdling scream remains muffled behind the tape. I was using it to make sure he didn't bleed out too fast, but waking his ass up is a nice bonus.

I rip the duct tape from his mouth and he yells, "you sick bit... gchgt." His words are interrupted as I shove one of his balls in his mouth and retape it. His eyes water, and I know he knows that he's going to die sucking on his own hairy ball.

Then I laugh an uncontrollable laugh that veers on almost hysterically. "Yeah, you don't need to finish that statement. I've heard it before."

"I'm done" I say to the others that are standing outside my kill room. I plunge a knife into his heart and take off the raincoat I am wearing to keep from being splashed with blood and step out of the plastic curtain.

"Fuck. It's a bloody mess in here." One of the guys says, "remind me never to piss her off."

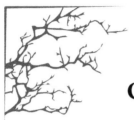

Chapter 50: Ace

A few days later...

"Stop being such a big baby," Storm says, as she crawls up on the bed. "I need you Ace, I want to feel you inside me, and I always get what I want."

I'm not going to pretend my leg isn't hurting from being shot, but her words has my cock swelling. I'm not about to stop where this is going. She slides her hand down my boxers and wraps it around my half-hard cock and brings her lips to mine.

"I'm going to ride you like you've never been ridden before," she purrs, as she works my boxers down to my knees.

I situate myself to make it easier for her to straddle me. "Please, do show me how you ride, Mrs. Prez." Gripping her hips, I pull her to me and lick the seam of her lips. She opens up, allowing me access and our warm wet tongues massage each others. I kiss her harder, biting her lip as I let her go. She lifts herself off from me and positions herself over my dick. Her wetness coats my shaft, letting her glide onto my cock, easily.

"Dollface, you are so wet," I groan, as she rides my cock like she's at a rodeo and I'm her bull.

"You like that don't ya? You like when I take what I want? You like when I fuck you." A smile shows on her face and she knows I don't mind giving her control sometimes. It's hot being with a woman that isn't afraid to be herself in the bedroom. When she knows how to satisfy herself and me at the same time.

"I fucking love it." I stick my fingers into her mouth, wanting her to get them wet for me. She glides her tongue around them, soaking them before I pull them out. She looks at me with hungry eyes before I rub her clit and make her fall apart as she continues to fuck herself on my cock. I hold her hips, hard enough to leave bruises. "That's it, Dollface, come for me," I coax as she arches her back. Her lips form an O and her eyes close in euphoria.

"I love the look on your face as you orgasm it's sexy as fuck." I slam my hips up and move my fingers at the same time causing her to come undone further. Before I know what's happening, Storm pulls her nine millimeter out from under a pillow and holds it between my eyes.

"Storm, what the fuck?" I scream, trying to move her off of me.

"Abbadon wasn't the last man that owes me vengeance, Ace, you are. Your daddy's life for yours, remember?" She thumbs the hammer. "I love you Talon." She kisses my lips, then bites it hard, causing a sharp sting. Warm blood trickles down my chin and copper explodes on my tongue, and then she pulls the trigger.

The click sounds, and I wait for the pain. The flash back moment throughout my life. I knew this was going to happen, but I wasn't sure of when or how. When the pain doesn't come, I open my eyes and I see Storm cracking up laughing. "You're crazy as fuck," I say, as she wipes tears of her laughter from her face.

"You wouldn't have me another way," she states, climbing off my now limp dick and slides beside me. "I'll make it up to you I promise."

"If you're going to kill me, Storm. Do it now," I plead, looking at her. "I don't want to wonder when or if it's going to happen."

"Ace, my Talon, my best friend, my love. I'm not going to kill you." She kisses my cheek. "We are going to make lots of babies. I'm going to be your ol' lady and you're gonna ride bitch on my bike until we are old and gray."

"Does that mean you're giving up being President of Daughters of Doom?" I ask, gazing into her eyes.

"You've lost your Goddamn mind! They are my sisters! You'll have to deal with us in Kentucky, share the area. Because, my girls and I are going to stay," she states, in a matter-of-fact tone. "Besides I think Chyna and Zeus are fucking."

-The end for now.

Milton Keynes UK
Ingram Content Group UK Ltd.
UKHW010932231123
433129UK00001B/94